ALL MY SINS

ALL MY SINS

a novel

DARYL SNEATH

$|$ N$_1$ $|$ O$_2$ $|$ N$_1$
CANADA

Library and Archives Canada Cataloguing in Publication

Sneath, Daryl, 1975–, author
All my sins / Daryl Sneath.

ISBN 978–1–926942–61–2 (pbk.)

I. Title.

PS8637.N43A55 2014   C813'.6   C2013–906592–X

Printed and bound in Canada on 100% recycled paper.

Now Or Never Publishing
#313, 1255 Seymour Street
Vancouver, British Columbia
Canada V6B 0H1

nonpublishing.com
Fighting Words.

We acknowledge the support of the Canada Council
for the Arts for our publishing program.

For my mom & my sister—for my gramma & poppa

For Ethan, Penelope, & Abigael

For Tara

Either Good or Bad

'Shakespeare should have ended the play with Hamlet's final words. But the end is never where we want it. The way something ends—such as life or love—can be as unpredictable and removed from reason as the way it begins.'

I was sitting-slash-leaning sideways against the desk at the front of the room when I said this, one knee up, shoulders square to the class. Like I was getting my picture taken. I read in Teacher Man that it's a more confident looking pose than the one where you keep both feet on the ground, hands clasped in your lap. Hard to tell, though, when you're the one posing. Regardless, it's a limited posture. I don't see it working in any other stage-like context.

Take being in a band for example. You certainly couldn't set up like this behind a mic and gain the same effect. Not unless you were doing something slow and lyrical. Maybe if you had a stool and you could put a foot up on a rung. Maybe if you were doing country. Maybe if you were Johnny Cash.

I wish I were Johnny Cash. I'd have no problems then. There's no way the principal gives Johnny Cash the hook when he's in the middle of a lesson on Hamlet. But let's just say she did—here's how I picture him handling it. All calm and black-attired, sitting-slash-leaning against the desk at the front of the room, one knee up, shoulders square to the class, saying something about flights of angels when the principal walks right in, two policemen in her wake, looming in the doorway. He'd turn, coolly unhurried, and after glancing at the authorities look right at the principal and say something like, 'Tell me you've found the smokin' gun, I'll stand and tell you I'm the one. But if all you've come on is a hunch and a whim, I ain't gonna move a solitary limb.' The class would roar and bang the desks even as Mr. Cash was directed to his feet and escorted from the room, hands drawn without protest behind his back and cuffed.

Let me clarify. I don't really wish I were Johnny Cash. Not in a literal sense. There's no point in that kind of wishing. Besides, he wasn't a man without his share of troubles. What I do wish[1] is that I'd made it as a musician.

But there's no point in that kind of wishing either, I know. What's the line from Dead Poets? 'Show me the heart unfettered by stupid dreams and I'll show you a happy man.' That's not it exactly, but it's close. Part of me wishes I could've been more like Mr. Keating, but there's no way someone gets away with teaching like that. Would've been nice, though, if a few students had stood on their desks and called out, 'O Captain, My Captain,' when the principal and her two heavies came in and escorted me away.

Anyway, as for my music career, I guess it was a stupid dream.

I gave it a go though. Back in undergrad I was in a band called The River's Edge. We were good, I think. About a year ago— before my inglorious removal from the high school—we got together for a reunion gig in Heron River. Where I used to live and teach. It was a send-off for Booker, our bassist and resident sage. A send-off for all of us, really. One last hurrah. We all knew without saying that this was it. Life was beginning to happen. Whatever that was supposed to mean. We wouldn't see much of each other over the next few years. Maybe ever. Not in the same way, at least, and not as frequently as we had at one time. We'd been a tight group during a period in our lives that couldn't last. We knew that. And now each of us was heading his own way.

How did Booker put it? 'Time for dis band to disband.'

Our sagacious bassist, Sheldon Booker, off to MUN for gradu-ate work in philosophy. He'd taken six years to finish undergrad but not because he didn't do well. Quite simply he didn't want to stop. His old man was Professor Emeritus in the Lit Department and so his tuition was covered. He was in no hurry. Why province hop all the way to MUN when you can go to school ad infini-tum (ad nauseam) on the house? Scholarships, for one—enough that he'd actually come out a little in the black—but more because he'd been in love with Newfoundland from afar for years.

---

[1] Aside from you reading this and walking back into my life.

He'd finally summoned the courage to ask her out and to his delight she'd said yes.

Also heading his own way was Emerson McKnight, our drummer. He was up to his eyeballs in a pile of real life stuff: wedding plans, taking over the family restaurant (an upscale spot called McKnight's in Heron River), and catechism classes. Elizabeth Anne—no short forms, thank you very much—was Catholic. His love for her, he told me, had also brought him a love for Jesus.

Jesus.

Anyway, hard for me to understand, but who am I to judge.[2]

Which brings me to Wyatt Stone, my childhood best friend who I've known, or so I thought, for some twenty years. How can you be best friends with a guy for that long and not know he putts from the rough? How many conversations had we had over the years about women and getting laid? Easier question: how many had we not? And now I find out he's gay. Don't get me wrong. I'm a liberal guy. I am. I mean I have other gay friends. Okay, not friends but acquaintances. Okay, not acquaintances, but I know their names and on occasion I've said hello.

Listen, I understand I'm not supposed to have a problem with homosexuality in this day and age. And I don't. Believe me. 'The state has no business in the bedrooms of the nation.' Trudeau said this forty years ago and it still ruffles the feathers of the Christian rightwingers today. Let's be clear: ideologically left of centre and spiritually ambivalent is where I'm most comfortable. So it's not like I disagree with Wyatt's lifestyle on a moral or religious or right-vs-wrong level. Not at all. Sex is sex. Love is love. As long as it's mutual.

What I have a problem with is that I feel like I don't know him. That's what upsets me most. How can you not know someone after, well, *knowing* him for twenty years? Okay. The argument is that he's still the same person. I know that. It's what he told me right after he informed me about his new, not-so-new lifestyle.

---

[2] I remember you teasing me one time for using the word 'whom.' I haven't used it since.

He said, 'It's still me, Ben. I'm no different.'

I looked at him and said, 'Fuck me, Wyatt, and please don't take that literally, but that's exactly what you are. Different.'

Sure, he's still him. Physically he's the same person. He's still Wyatt. When someone calls out his name, he's the one to respond. (Men call out his name. *Men* for Christ sake. Maybe it's always been men. Maybe all those women were just beards. Maybe he likes beards. Jesus. Beards, can you imagine?) But let's be honest. He's not the same. He is the very definition of different. In every sense of the word. Here's one sense: abnormal. And I don't mean this as a judgment. I mean it quite literally. Etymologically 'off' or 'away from' normal. He's different from the majority of men whose main reason for existence is to knuckle-drag this earth in search of mates, physically driven by their cock-probing, evolutionary impulse to reproduce. He doesn't have that drive. He's driven to spread his seed, sure, but not on fertile ground. He spreads it 'where the sun don't shine,' the good old boys from home might say. If he were a farmer it wouldn't matter how much seed he sowed—none of it would catch and away she'd blow (in his case, *he'd*). Not a single bit of life would come from his sowing. The powers that be would seize everything he owned. He'd starve.

Again, I know how this must sound. I'm sorry. This isn't really me. Hickish, I mean. But I told myself when I sat down to write this thing that I wouldn't censor what I wrote. I'm trying to be honest. For practical reasons in addition to the ethical ones. Practical because I haven't decided yet what this is—a memoir or a novel.[3] If it's a memoir it's supposed to be true (meaning 'factual,' I guess) in all its major component parts, which is the only significant difference I can see between the two genres. Memoirs are true. Novels are not.

At any rate, just in case I decide to call it a memoir, I'm not going to censor or embellish anything. (I wouldn't want to get in trouble with Oprah. Imagine.) So what I mean to do here is relate

---

[3] Believe it or not it started out as a letter to you but it's already too long for that and I'm nowhere near the apology part.

what has happened to me in the last little while, with a few necessary forays into the not too distant past, and in so doing, come to some understanding, myself, of how all this unfolded the way it did.[4]

Ultimately I am responsible for what happens to me. I know that. But I think Wyatt's 'little something to tell you' played at least a minor role in me sleeping with Chantal Aster that critical night last August, which in turn played at least a minor role in me getting fired. (That's what he called it: *a little something to tell you.* Standing at the bar, clinking pints between sets on our last night as a band—our last hurrah—he looked at me and said, 'Ben, buddy, I have a little something to tell you. And I hope you're not too upset. I hope it won't change anything.')

I'm not blaming him for Chantal. At the time I didn't think I was doing anything wrong. I still don't, to be honest. I think unconsciously (there's an interesting phrase: 'think unconsciously'), if I were to psychoanalyze myself, part of what made me take Chantal home that night was that I wanted to confirm my own staunch heterosexuality. If my best friend had secretly been playing for the other team all these years, what did that make me?

Here. This is how it felt. When Wyatt told me he was gay. It was like finding out Darryl Sittler or Dougie Gilmour used to sit at home on off nights with Habs jerseys on, drinking *la fin du monde* from quart bottles (I know, *la fin du monde* didn't come out until '94 but that's not the point), leaping from their couches, shouting, 'C'est le but! C'est le but!' whenever Lafleur or Vinney Damphousse dumped one in the net.

Anyway, since Wyatt was my best friend, other players on my team might start to question where my loyalties lie. And I didn't want that. I wanted everyone (including myself) to know where I stood—more accurately, where I lay. I had a reputation and I wanted to keep it.

So just as Wyatt opened his closet door and went to take a step towards me, I slammed it in his face. What was I supposed to do, shake his hand, give him a big back-slapping man-hug for

---

[4] The main component of 'all this' being how I've ended up without you.

being so brave, so true to himself, then share a laugh and tell him, 'No worries, man, at least you still have good taste in music'? I couldn't do it. I just couldn't. I know I should have. It would have been the best friend thing to do. But in the moment, when I looked at him and saw his pathetic it's-still-me, puppy-begging eyes waiting for me to tell him it was alright, to embrace him with unqualified acceptance and fraternal love, all I could picture was him dropping to his knees and offering me a conciliatory blowjob. It made me sick. I mean physically sick. Like I had to retch. So I said the line about him being different (which really wasn't all that bad, considering), turned, and left him standing there at the bar. That was a year ago and save for the one brief encounter I haven't spoken to him since.

All I could think about was getting laid. I could hear this little voice in my head saying, 'Dunn, man, you need to get laid. Tonight. I mean, you really need to. Just to make sure.' Stupid, I know, but honest.

I was heading back to the stage for our last set when I felt a tap on my shoulder.

Our *last* last set. Ever. I hate to digress again, but really. What a fucker. Why didn't he wait until the end of the night to tell me? Why'd he have to tell me at all? Here's a question for Booker: why are we so conditioned to tell those who are closest to us *everything* about us, even when we know that what we tell them might ruin things forever? This I know: there's nothing evolutionary about honesty.

Anyway, I thought it was Wyatt tapping me on the shoulder, wanting either to plead with me one more time, saying, 'It's still me, Ben—nothing has changed,' or, just as likely, 'You know what? Fuck you, Ben. I don't need you anyway.' Regardless, I didn't want to hear it, so I swung around, swiping the hand from my shoulder, and stuck a finger in the face of the tapper, ready to tell him to get his hands the fuck off me, I wasn't some goddamn tunnel dweller like him, couldn't he see that? So fuck right off and leave me alone. But just as I was about to let loose, she—not he, not Wyatt—reached up and took my gun-barrel finger in her hand and shook it.

So cool. So not eighteen.

Grinning, she said, 'Didn't your mother ever teach you that pointing is rude?'

Without pause, without even thinking, I furrowed my brow and said, 'I haven't seen my mother since I was three. She left without a trace, which sucked the life right out of my father and turned him into a ghost. She didn't teach me anything except how to forget. So.'

Her eyes got big and she nodded once. 'Okay. Well.'

She drew a hand through her hair and went to step by me. I stopped her. A hand on her shoulder. She didn't resist.

'I don't know why I said all that. I'm sorry. Let me start again.'

I was trying to keep my eyes on her face when I spoke. Not glancing down was almost impossible. She had on a pair of snug, low-cut jeans and a tight white tank top casually but purposefully hiked up a little, showing off her tanned midriff and silver belly button piercing. I knew without looking that there was a tiny butterfly tattoo fluttering up the small of her back from below her belt.

'It's just, you caught me at kind of a weird moment. Everything's spinning.'

'Probably shouldn't drink so much.'

I grinned. 'Hard to resist when they pay you in beer.'

'You're like Johnny Cash. You know, minus all the black garb and the voice of course.'

I looked at her. She grinned.

'Hard to tell with some people, isn't it?'

'What.'

'If they're being serious.'

'Yes—I mean, no. I could tell. With you.'

She looked over her shoulder at nothing in particular, then back at me. I wanted to say something clever about needing her to help me confirm my manhood, but we weren't there yet. If I'd been Booker I would have said something like, 'Listen, I'll be honest. I don't know you and you don't know me, but I find myself in a bit of a predicament and I believe very strongly that the gods of yore have sent you here as an angel of delicate beauty to wrench me from the muck and mire I'm in. You see, I desperately need to confirm something and I'd be ever so grateful if you assisted me in acquiring this confirmation. To be quite plain, I need to confirm my heterosexuality and for this task I do require your assistance. What do you say?'

He actually talked like this when he wanted to and got away with it. Most people could never tell if he was being serious or not.

She spoke next. 'So.'

'So.'

'Why do people say *so* like that? *So*. It's not what they mean.'

'I don't know. Why *do* they say it? Why did *you* say it?'

'*They* say it because they don't like awkward silences. *I* said it because you were looking at me like you had something to say. *You* said it because I said it.'

'Oh.'

'See? There's another one. *Oh*.'

I looked over my shoulder at nothing in particular and scratched the back of my head. When I looked at her again she was smirking.

'So. Back to your spinning.'

'My spinning.'

'You had a little love spat. I know how it is.'

'Love spat.'

'Your boyfriend. Looked pretty serious.'

I checked the bar. Wyatt was gone. I felt sick again.

I shook my head. Emphatically. 'Christ no. We're just friends. *Were*.'

'Oh. By the way he was looking at you, I just thought—and on stage, the two of you just seemed so—'

'So what?'

She shook her head. 'I'm kidding.'

We went quiet but it wasn't awkward.

'You know, you look a lot like someone I know.'

She nodded, grinned. 'How's that usually work out for you?'

'How does what usually work out for me?'

'That line.'

'It's not a line. Really. It's the truth.'[5]

'Truth? I'm more of a dare girl.'

'I could've guessed that.'

'So dare me.'

'Okay—I dare you to come up on stage.'[6]

'On stage.'

She put a hand on my arm, rocked towards me, and bounced a little.

'Seriously?'

'Seriously.'

'OhmygodI'dloveto.'[7]

All I could think about was slipping her tanktop over her head.

'So.'

'So.'

She grabbed my shirt and sort of pulled me, which moved her more than it did me. 'You can be Johnny. I'll be June.'

'Cute.'

'I wasn't going for cute.'

Still holding my shirt, she stood on her toes and stared at my mouth. I leaned in.

'It ain't me, babe.'

I waited.

'That's the song we'll do. You know—' she sang the next bit '—it ain't me you're looking for, babe.'

'Listen. I think it *is* you I'm looking for. If you want to know the truth.'

She bit her bottom lip.

'Remember, I'm a dare girl. Truth is never as fun.'

She kissed me and turned to leave.

'Wait. We didn't do names.'

---

[5] I couldn't believe how much she looked like you.

[6] I thought of the night we met in Windsor. When I convinced you to come up and sing Eileen Aaroon.

[7] Okay. She sounded eighteen here. And sort of looked it when she bounced up and down. But it was too late.

'I know who you are, Mr. Dunn.'[8]

'Please. Call me Ben.'

She smirked.

'Okay, Ben. Dunn.'

She stepped towards me, pulled herself up by my shirt again, and whispered in my ear, 'But you haven't been done by me yet.'

Jesus.

She let go of my shirt and moved away, still looking at me. 'In case you're wondering, I'm Chantal Aster. You know, like a song and a star.'

I nodded.

Like a song and a star.

---

[8] I should've known right then.

As a teacher, I was supposed to be morally upstanding. A pillar of goodness, whatever the hell that meant. But the doctors of education, in all their erudite pedagogical wisdom, didn't get into that sort of thing in Teacher's College. I think they must have assumed it to be innate in anyone who endeavours to stand at the front of a classroom for a living and therefore found it unnecessary to address or discuss in any formal manner.

Big mistake.

Another thing I was supposed to have, I soon found out, was stage presence. Which I should have been able to take from my days with The River's Edge, but standing at the front of a classroom—all alone, no band behind you, under the light of day—is a lot different from belting out songs atop a little stage at the front of an overcrowded bar of drunk-happy singalongers and would-be groupies. And much scarier if you ask me.

Maybe it was fear that led to my downfall. Everything started to unravel after Wyatt told me what he told me. It wasn't long after that I found out about the video of me allegedly selling marijuana to a student. Imagine. I mean, sure, I smoked a little now and then. Who didn't? But I never sold it. Especially not to students. The powers that be had evidence, yes, but it was manufactured and taken out of context. And the six supplemental testimonies they had all came from students who had either failed my class or, for one reason or another, had it in for me. I tried to explain this to the principal and her associate boys in blue, but they weren't having any of it. The video trumped anything I said. In any event—and my extraction from the classroom was certainly an event—it didn't matter now. It was too late. The damage was done and there was certainly no undoing it.

(*Aside.* I don't know why some words exist. Like 'undoing.' Once something is done there is no undoing the doing of it. Nothing can be undone. Except maybe laces when they accidentally lose their knottedness. So I guess I'm like laces. I've lost my knottedness. I've come undone. 'Hello everyone. I'm Ben. Un–Dunn.')

I needed to talk to Booker. He'd know what to say. He always did. Which is amazing when you think about it. How one person can always know what to say.

I called him and told him about my removal from the school. He seemed neither shocked nor concerned in any way. Classic Booker.

He said, 'Well, Ben Franklin, I wouldn't worry too much about what comes and goes. There's a tendency for things to right themselves. Blue skies are imminent. Survival is a certainty.'

'How's Ireland for blue skies?'

'I wouldn't know. Why?'

'That's where I'm going. There really isn't anything keeping me here anymore.'

I knew he wouldn't take offence. He wasn't *here* anyway. He was in St. John's. Besides, what I really meant was there was something drawing me *there*, to Ireland. Dun Laoghaire to be exact. And had been for years.

Booker said, 'Does she know?'

'Sort of. We promised we'd see each other again.'

'And that was . . . ?'

'Seven years ago.'

'Seven years ago. Hmn. I'd probably call first.'

'You think I'm stupid.'

'You're not stupid, Ben.'

'Still, it's crazy. She won't even remember me.'

'I don't know.'

'She's probably married. With kids.'

'It's possible.'

'She might not even be there anymore.'

'No, she mightn't be.'

'You're right. It's crazy.'

'I didn't say it was crazy.'

'No, but you keep agreeing with me.'

'Not really.'

'Well, you're not disagreeing with me.'

'No.'

'So what are you saying?'

'I'm not really saying anything.'

'Jesus, Booker.'

'What.'

'Well fuck, man, should I go or shouldn't I?'

'I can't tell you that.'

'Why not? I'm asking you to. I'm asking you to tell me.'

'No man knows anything about another man's *should* or *shouldn't*.'

He was right, of course, but all I wanted was for him to say I should pack my bags and go, send me on my way with a little bon voyage aphorism about living for the moment.

'Okay, you're right. Fundamentally, you're right. But listen, Booker, I'm asking for a little shove here. An innocuous little nudge.'

'And what if I give you this little nudge and then you discover, coming out of the fog you're in, that all the while you were standing at the edge of a cliff.'

'That'll be my problem.'

'And mine for having been the one to push.'

'Come on, man, I just need something with a little carpe diem in it.'

'I'll tell you this, even though deep within I know you already know it.' He cleared his throat. 'To dare is to lose one's footing momentarily. Not to dare is to lose oneself entirely.'

Dare. Yes, Goddamnit. Go on and dare, Dunn. Be a man. Truth is never as fun.

I was in Dun Laoghaire in less than a week.

It was that bastard, Grant Richards, who made the video. One of those time-martying, do-everything-by-the-letter men who somehow still wind up ineffectual in everything they are and do.

Except in setting me up. He did that well. Exceedingly well.

A+. Level 4. Grant has demonstrated a superior knowledge and understanding of the curricular concepts regarding the destruction of another human life.

I knew well enough from the outset that he didn't like me—one of the easiest things in this life is to be able to tell when someone doesn't like you—but I didn't know his contempt reached so far beyond the normal level of contempt that he would go to the trouble of producing a slanderous, albeit amateur, biopic of me and then screen the premiere behind closed doors in the principal's office, special invite to the local fuzz.

The first day of school last September I stopped him in the hall and said, 'Hey there, Terry, how goes it? How was your summer?'

Too bad I never had a mother around to tell me the better man always chooses to be nice. It might have saved me a lot of embarrassment. Not to mention a job. There. We'll blame her. We'll blame the absent mother. That's what the psychologists would do.

Anyway, Richards had no idea why I called him Terry which—coupled with my diction-compromised greeting—pissed him off royally.

He furrowed his brow.

'My name, Mr. Dunn, is not Terry. It is Grant, which you know very well. And I prefer Mr. Richards, as I have told you before, particularly in the professional setting in which we are in. I do believe I have earned it.'

Tsk, tsk. One too many *ins*, Terry.

'Of course. Sorry, Grant. I mean Mr. Richards. Jesus, I'm awful like that. It's just, you remind me of this Terry guy I know. Anyway, sorry.'

'Mm-hmn.'

He crossed his arms and looked down his nose at me.

'Yeah. So. Anyway, I wanted to ask if you'd ever heard of a writer by the name of Rickler.'

'You mean *Richler*.'

'Yeah, that's the guy.'

'That *guy*, Mr. Dunn, is only one of our most important literary treasures.'

'Really. He's Canadian. Huh.'

Richards closed his eyes, squeezed the bridge of his nose, muttered something. I leaned in.

'What's that?'

He looked at me. 'I think you mean, *Pardon*.'

'Huh?'

I couldn't resist.

He sighed, shook his head. 'Never mind, Mr. Dunn.'

'Okay. So. Back to Rickler.'

'Richler.'

'Yeah, sure. Whatever.'

'You do know, Mr. Dunn, that The Apprenticeship of Duddy Kravitz is on the grade ten academic course, which you are scheduled to teach yourself next semester.'

He pronounced Duddy like 'duty' and scheduled like 'shed-jewelled.' If he'd meant 'teach yourself' like I had to actually *teach* myself the novel it would've been funny.

'Kravitz. Right. Great book. A man without land is nobody.'

'I think you mean, a man without land is no *one*, Mr. Dunn.'

Nope. I checked. It shows up more often as 'nobody.' Just to note.

'I knew you'd know a bunch about him, Terry.'

He squinted.

'I mean, Grant. Shit. Sorry. Mr. Richards. God, I'm awful. I have to try to remember that—Mr. Richards. Mr. Richards.'

He closed his eyes again, collected himself.

'You know, Mr. Dunn, despite your seemingly intentional insensitivity, I am curious as to why you asked me about Richler.'

'Oh. Yeah. Right. Well, I saw something about him on the news the other night and instantly thought of you. They were talking about Canadian Literature and film. I know how much you like that sort of thing, so I said to myself, Dunn, I bet if you asked Grant—I mean Mr. Richards—he'd have something interesting to say about it.'

He folded his arms. 'Yes. You are correct. I am interested in that sort of thing.'

'Well, I didn't catch it all, but they've turned one of his books into a movie. Benny's Story, I think it was called.'

'You mean, Barney's Version.'

'Huh?'

He shut his eyes again.

'The title of the novel to which you are referring is Barney's Version. Not Benny's Story.'

'Oh. Yeah. Right. Barney's Version. That's it.'

'So?'

'So what?'

'So what about it, Mr. Dunn?'

'Oh. Yeah. Right. I just wanted to know what you thought about them turning his book into a movie.'

'I have yet to see this particular film. But if I had to guess, it is a mistake.'

'A mistake, eh? Why, book no good?'

He shook his head, sighed again. 'No, Mr. Dunn. The book is very good. Many—and I am referring now to those who have an educated, informed, worthwhile opinion on the matter— consider it to be Richler's finest work. I am partial to The Apprenticeship myself, but I think that may be because I have taught it so many times. I have experienced it on all its various levels, which of course heightens the enjoyment and understanding of a work of literature.' He crossed his arms. 'You do know what I am referring to when I say *levels*, don't you, Mr. Dunn?'

Oh, Terry, watch your preposition placement. I think you meant ' . . . to what I am referring . . .' And that wasn't a contraction I heard, was it?

'Oh. Yeah. Right. Levels. Like in that Seinfeld episode when Kramer wants to put them in his apartment, with steps and carpet and pillows. Like ancient Egypt.'

Richards clenched his fists. He was burning. He managed to collect himself, man that he is, before he turned and left.

'Terry. Terry. Come on now. Don't go away mad. I was only kidding.'

I stretched my arms out towards him as he walked away.

'Mr. Richards. Please. Tell me about the levels. I want to know about the levels.'

What a prick I am. I had it coming I guess. What he did to me.

During my stint as a teacher, the Celtic Pub down on River Street called The Banjo & Axe became the site of my mind-saving Friday afternoon sessions with the Disgruntled Heads. The Old Guard, as it were. The ones who ran the show but at the same time were the first and last to mock it. A group of acerbic veterans who were only a couple of years away from retirement, which was, so they claimed, the only thing still fuelling their engines. They told it how it was and I liked the way they told it, their innocuous but genuine, cut-to-the-quick brand of cynicism. Something to aspire to. They were so much easier to be around than the self-absorbed, whiny, would-be pedagogues of my own generation who sighed with every breath and went on about how much they had to do, forever fishing for sympathy and back-patting, passively but ceaselessly soliciting recognition for their selfless, brilliant work. Work, if you could call it that, which was no different from anyone else's. Conditioned since birth, this generation of mine, to walk around with their ears peeled for praise, expecting accolades for every little thing they managed to do on their own. Oh look, he drank from a cup and didn't spill a drop, big round of applause. See there, he wiped his own ass clean, just like a pro, standing ovation.

They brought it on themselves as far as I could tell. All their so-called work. I really think they did much of what they did simply so they could say they had done it. *Oh, you wouldn't believe how long it took me to mark those tests last night. I read them all first, you know, as we should, to get a general feel for how each of the students did with respect to one another, you know, in order to be as fair as possible, and I made certain to make comments on each answer so that every student might understand where she went wrong. There were a few blanks here and there but I didn't mark those. I gave the student the benefit of the doubt, as we should. You can't penalize someone for not seeing a question or forgetting to go back to it. A missed question has nothing to do with what they know and should have nothing to do with our assessment of them. It wouldn't be fair. So in the end everyone got at least a B—Yay! (clap, clap)—which made me so happy. Like I'm really doing my job, you know? It's such a good feeling when you become an integral part, however small, of student success. I've heard other teachers say they can't get this group to do anything. They use words like 'hellions' and 'slugs'—isn't that awful? I mean, really, what a thing to say about your students. Anyway, they seem to work well for me, whatever the reason. It's not without effort, though, let me tell you. I was up till three in morning last night. I wanted to customize these writing prompts on the computer. You can't just write on the board anymore. It's not the same. They've done studies. I really believe in differentiated delivery. It just makes sense. After all, our job is to engage the students. We have to make it fun and interesting. Otherwise why would they want to learn? Why would anyone? It's worth the extra effort. So tell me, and give me your honest opinion, what do you think of these? Aren't they wonderful? I've tried to reflect the emotion of what each prompt says by using particular fonts and colours. It took me a while but I think I've got it right. You can borrow them if you like. I'd just ask that you be careful and return them when you're finished. They did take me a while. I can show you how, if you like.*

It's praise these teachers want, what they long for, what they give away unjustifiably to their students. If admiration be the food of life, laud on! Give me excess of it. They've been given excess of it their whole lives and so they can't get enough. They want it even more than money. Survey a panel of new teachers. Ask them if they'd rather earn an extra hundred bucks a paycheque or receive public approbation and be given a framed personalized Certificate of Recognition for all their self-sacrificing, dedicated hours of hard work. You'd be surprised how many pass on the pay-raise.

We are a generation addicted to the approval of others.

I say *we* because I was no better. I'm still not. I mean, I think I would've taken the hundred bucks, but still, I was part of the problem. I sought praise and approval just like the rest of them. I have to say, the DH was the best thing for me. I'm not sure how well I fit in—I was thirty years younger and I hadn't been teaching long enough to be justly disgruntled—but I'm pretty sure they were glad to have me.[9]

I remember the first Friday of my first week of teaching. I was sitting at my desk, staring at the school calendar, doing a mental count of the seventy-plus days to Christmas (something I never did as a student), shaking my head, thinking, *This gig ain't for me*, and I felt someone shake my chair. It was Norman Scott. Department Head to the stars. Tall, wide-shouldered, thick, likely a linebacker in his younger years. He had the kind of voice that rises above all others in a room and summons, without actually summoning, everyone's attention. He could've been in radio. From the first handshake you knew he was genuine. Warm, gentle, welcoming. Even in his sarcasm. Nothing fake about him. A bit clichéd with the corduroy jacket and tie, the pipe, the Sean Connery beard, but genuine just the same. Paternal without meaning or trying to be.

'It's Friday.'

'Huh?'

He didn't correct me. He didn't sigh either. 'You're staring at that calendar like it was a Mensa riddle.'

He pointed.

'See, we're here. Friday. End of the week. The weekend, as it's come to be known. I'll be brief. Dunn, my son, you're done.'

He was grinning. I nodded.

'I was just—'

'Counting the days to Christmas. Seventy-two, right?'

I looked up at him. He crossed his arms, winked.

'I don't know.'

'No, I'm quite sure. It's seventy-two.'

'No, I mean, I don't know—I don't know if this is for me.'

He laughed. 'This. What do you mean by *this*? This place, this job, this conversation, this quintessence of dust?'

He spoke to the ceiling and held an invisible fleck between the thumb and forefinger of his right hand.

---

[9] Although I'm not always the best judge of that. I thought the same thing of you.

He looked at me.

'This job, I guess. I mean, I don't know if I have what it takes.'

There I was, just like the rest of them. Fishing.

'Of course you don't. The only things you can be sure about from the get-go are drinking and sex.'

I grinned, sort of.

'Jesus, you're in a bad way.' He shook his head, crossed his arms. 'What are you, twenty-five?'

'Almost twenty-three.'

'Almost twenty-three and they managed to suck the laugh and the life out of you in a week. That must be one hell of a timetable you've got.'

Thinking back on it now, he must have known the hell that was my timetable since he had a major hand in giving it to me. All grade ten Applied (what used to be known as 'General' or whatever other label that means 'not academic'), ninety percent boys, more than fifty percent identified behavioural (slamming doors, fighting, spitballs, lighters under desks, looking right at the teacher and telling him without hesitation or reserve to go fuck himself. The usual.) An initiation of sorts, I would later learn.

He took me by the arm, pulled me out of the chair. 'Let's go. You're coming with me.'

It felt a little like I was being arrested (something I can now speak to). He held my arm all the way down the hall and out into the parking lot. He even opened the car door and guided me into the seat as if I were cuffed.

He took forty bucks from his wallet and gave it to me. 'Here. Buy a round. They'll like that.'

When I went to say something he slapped me on the knee and cranked the radio. He squeezed his eyes shut and sang along: 'The child is grown, the dream is done, and I have become . . . comfortably numb.' Then, just before peeling away, he looked at me, all jokingly serious, and said, 'Stay away from the drugs, son.'

The last time I saw him was about a week after the principal and her two heavies escorted me from my classroom. He came over to the apartment to tell me he didn't believe any of what they were accusing me of and said I shouldn't give in so easily. Maybe I should've listened.

Soon after ripping out of the parking lot that first Friday afternoon I was in the back of The Banjo & Axe being introduced to the other members of the DH.

We walked up to the booth and Norman presented me. 'Gentlemen,' he said, 'this is Ben Dunn.'

The one called Smitty looked shocked and incredulous. 'This hasn't been done. Has this been done? When was this done?'

It didn't take long to catch on to the tone of the table.

Norman said, 'He's new.'

The one called Marty laughed. 'Really. I'd never have guessed.' He scanned me. 'Twenty-five?'

Norman raised his brow. 'Almost twenty-three.'

Marty laughed again.

Norman continued. 'And he tells me—he tells me he doesn't know about this.'

Marty took a mouthful of beer. 'No one knows about *this*. *This* doesn't matter. It's *that* you have to worry about.'

The last one, the biggest and least teacher-looking of the group, banged the table with a fist. Loud enough to make me jump. He glared at me.

'Bug.'

I didn't know if it was a threat, a warning, an announcement of an actual kill, or all three. No one said anything. Norman put a hand to his mouth and whispered, 'Big Joe.'

Big Joe continued to stare at me. 'I hate a bug,' he said, and I thought he said, *I ate a bug*.

I looked at Norman. Straight-faced, he raised his brow and shrugged. Smitty and Marty did the same when I looked at them.

Big Joe stared and stared, his fist still clenched. Without notice he slapped the table with an open hand and laughed. He roared and looked at each of the other men. They were all laughing too. I didn't know what to make of it at first. It was like that scene from Goodfellas when Pesci gets all serious and says, 'Whaddya mean I'm funny? Funny how? Funny like I amuse you? Like I'm a clown?' and then after a moment of uncertain tension Ray Liotta erupts in mad laughter. That's what it was like. I didn't know whether to join in or to piss myself.

Still going, Big Joe pointed at me. 'Christ, you should've seen your face.'

Norman clapped both hands on my shoulders and shook me a little. He pulled out a chair for himself and one for me. 'Have a seat,' he said. 'Have a seat.'

I nodded and sat. Then I remembered the forty bucks Norman had given me. I raised my hand, caught the bartender's eye, and gestured for another round. He nodded and started filling pints.

Big Joe extended a hand across the table. He was grinning. We shook. He could've crushed my hand if he'd wanted to.

'Welcome to the Disgruntled Heads,' he said. 'You can be our water boy.'

Everyone laughed again. I was smiling. This was my kind of table.

.   .   .

The DH wasn't much for rules. In fact they loathed them. The practice of them and even more the notion of them. But like everyone else in the free world they couldn't get around the fact that rules existed. Which meant they had to at least pretend to abide by the ones that applied to them.

'Similar,' Marty said, 'to the way we accept the necessity to coexist non-violently with stupid people.'

Norman said, 'We don't have the energy, the will, or the means for an uprising.'

'We prefer to drink copious amounts of beer, clandestinely flout said rules, and mock the stupid people we have to coexist with behind their stupid backs.'

Big Joe grunted, used his caveman voice: 'Me hate stupid people.'

Again, I thought he said *ate*—*I ate stupid people*. Which wouldn't have surprised me.

'Listen,' Norman said, 'in all seriousness, don't be cocky or careless about breaking the rules you choose to break and you'll be fine. Go about your business how you see fit and no one will bother you. Start making a show of how you're a rebel without a cause and the effect will be Eckleburg's eyes glued to your every move. And you don't want that. A life of 'Yes, sir, no sir. Oh, I'm so sorry, sir. Can I please powder your ass, sir. Except she's not a sir. She's a ma'am. Which makes it even worse.'

They called the principal Eckleburg. Her real name was Trudy J. Eckerton (what are the odds?) and she had at least half a dozen ornate, face-defining frames which she wore according to the power suit she happened to have on that day.

Although they detested rules, there was one in particular they insisted the table abide by: no shop talk. Big Joe banged the table when I asked what department each of them ran. In a straight, no-joke sort of voice, he pointed at me and said, 'Kid. I'll tell you one time. We don't talk about that place in here.'

I'll be honest. He frightened me.

'Sorry. I didn't mean to—'

'No sorrys either.'

Not so much a rule as an attitude. I nodded and drank my beer.

Although 'no shop talk' was their only rule, everyone but Big Joe made an exception for me that first night.

Marty clapped his hands once. 'Okay. Let's get this out of the way.'

I looked at him.

'When you say you're not sure about this, I assume *this* refers to the job.'

I nodded.

'That's what I thought. Here's my advice: don't be an idiot.'

He was looking right at me.

Norman jumped in. 'He means don't go fucking it up by thinking there's something better out there.'

Smitty shook his head. 'You won't find a better gig than this.'

'Hey!' Big Joe slammed the table.

'Knock it off, Joe. The kid needs a little professional help.'

Big Joe got up from the table. There were no exceptions for him.

'Don't mind Joe,' Norman said. 'He takes his disgruntledness very seriously.'

'So,' Smitty said. 'What's the problem here?'

I shook my head. 'I just don't think I have what it takes.'

'Idiot.'

I looked at Marty. He shrugged.

'If the shoe fits.'

'Listen,' Norman said, 'you think you stink, am I right? As a teacher, I mean.'

I nodded.

'You don't stink. Believe me, there are seasoned teachers whose malodorous efforts in the classroom are far worse than yours. Their seasoning, instead of preserving them, has done nothing to keep them from going rancid. Their stench permeates the halls and what's worse, they're not even aware of it. Like the kid whose B.O. stinks up every place he's in but he's so used to his own disgustingness that if anyone ever told him about the foul cloud he leaves in his wake he'd lift an arm, sniff, and say, What are you talking about? I don't stink.'

'But how do you know?'

'How do I know what?'

'That I don't stink.'

'We just know.'

'None of you have even seen me teach.'

Again, he could have corrected me but he didn't.

'Doesn't matter. Listen. We're not trying to puff you up. Just take our word for it and our advice. Be frustrated once in a while. Be sarcastic about students and cynical about the system, but don't whine.'

He looked at me. I nodded and that was the end of it.

'Now. Here's what you have to know about teaching. This is the only time you'll hear us talk about the profession in any kind of serious way. So listen.' He put the word 'profession' in finger-quotes.

Norman was the one to start and Marty and Smitty came in at even intervals. It was like a routine they had rehearsed.

'The worst thing you can do is distance yourself.'

'You'll never win them over that way.'

'And that's the name of the game these days.'

'Winning them over.'

'Used to be roles were clearly laid out.'

'Teacher, student.'

'My space, your space.'

'Yes sir, no sir.'

'Teaching was about information-giving.'

'And the provocation of thought.'

'Not anymore.'

'Now it's about information-sifting.'

'And the attempted generation of thought.'

'Clarification: they are *not* the Generation of Thought.'

'More like the Generation of Nought.'

'The My Space Generation.'

'And My Space is the exact opposite of what it used to be.'

'My Space is Everyone's Space.'

'Soon Your Space will be a site online.'

'Where you post pictures and opinions about other people.'

'Want to know what people really think about you? Visit your Your Space page.'

'Click here to register now!'

'Anyway, you have to let them get close enough to 'your space' to see that you're not *who* or *what* they think you are.'

'The job is to convince them of our humanness.'

'That's it.'

'To show them we understand where they're coming from.'

'To assure them our number one concern is to help them get where they want to go.'

'Even if it's not.'

'Even if they don't deserve it.'

'Which we'd never say of course.'

'Though it will be true much of the time.'

'Used to be we'd tell them how it was.'

'How it was going to be and how it wasn't.'

'No euphemisms.'

'Not anymore.'

'Here's the new job description: Bridge the gap.'

'Lower the bar.'

'Dumb it down.'

'That's it.'

'That's all there is to it.'

'And here's the new creed: Facilitators of dependence.'

'Enablers of mediocrity.'

'Architects of entitlement.'

'Hand holders.'

'Spoon feeders.'

'Punching bags are we.'

'What we're getting at is this: if you can stand up there day after day—'

'And just ride the river for what it is.'

'An obsolete, polluted passageway.'

'—then you'll make it to the end.'

'Don't get us wrong.'

'We enjoy the job.'

'As much as you can enjoy anything called a job.'

'There will be good moments along the way.'

'Just don't expect too much.'

'From yourself.'

'Or from them.'

'No one cares anymore if a student can recite a soliloquy.'

'We're happy these days if he can pronounce soliloquy.'

'And if he—'

'More likely she—'

'Happens to spell it right—'

'Fluke or not—'

'Call the press—'

'We have a gifted child on our hands.'

In unison, they sat back in their chairs and drank. I wanted to clap and say something like, *My God, gentleman, what a performance*, but it would've sounded stupid. So I just sat there and nodded. Like an idiot.

Big Joe returned with a fresh pint. Before sitting, he looked at Norman. 'So. You done?'

'We've already been over this, Joe. I'm Norman.' He grinned and flipped a thumb at me. 'This is Dunn.'

'Listen. Are you done or what?'

'You mean *finished*, Joe.'

Norman took a handful of peanuts from the dish on the table and popped them in his mouth one at time. Big Joe furrowed his brow. His whole face was tight.

'A man can't be done, Joe. Unless he's actually done. Which means he's dead. And none of us, as I'm sure you can tell, is dead. Really—as far as describing a living, breathing sort of man—he can only be finished.'

Anyone else talking like this to Big Joe would certainly have been finished. Or done.

Norman looked at Marty, then Smitty, then up at Big Joe. He reached out and slapped one of his legs. 'Come on, you big galoot. Have a seat. I'm just fucking with you. We're done—hah, I mean finished.'

Big Joe relented and took his seat. Norman caught the eye of our waiter walking by and ordered another round.

'So listen,' he said, setting his hands together, leaning his fore-arms on the table, 'I was reading this very interesting article the other day in Today's Teacher—'

He stopped and glanced at Big Joe.

'I hate Today's Teacher.'

I ate today's teacher.

Norman clapped Big Joe on the back and laughed. 'That a boy, Joe. That a boy.'

There are people in this world, I've learned, who can get away with anything.

(*Aside*. I'm not one of them.)

As I was saying at the beginning of all this, I was in the middle of my grade twelve English class when the principal came barging in, asking me to please come with her. It was one in the afternoon. We'd just finished Hamlet and I was trying to incite some kind of discussion around the significance of the Prince's dying words.

So there I was, sitting-slash-leaning against the desk at the front of the room, one knee up, shoulders square to the class, Mr. Teacher Man himself, pretentious-yet-genuine, embarking on what would be my very last discussion as a teacher without even knowing it.

'The most beautiful, mind-blowingly perfect words ever spoken at the moment of the grand exit—I mean in the history of the entire world—are those spoken by Hamlet.'

'And why is that, Dunn? Enlighten us.'

This was Dean. Everyone referred to him as The Dean. Which fit. He was the definition of smart. Not simply a rememberer of things, but a thinker. What's more, he could talk. He could take command of a room without really meaning or trying to. He reminded me of Booker.

'Why do you think, Dean?'

'Oh, come on, Dunn. Don't do that.'

'Don't do what?'

'That bullshit move where you throw the question back at the questioner. I don't see any couches in here.'

A few students laughed.

'Fair enough.'

'Ah, Dunn. There's no such thing as fair enough. Either something's fair or it's not. The only mitigating factor is a person's definition of fair. But there are no degrees. Just is just. Beautiful is beautiful. And in the end, there is nothing more beautiful than that which is just.'

Kendra, the redhead who sat at the front of the room, spun in her desk.

'What the hell are you talking about?'

Dean ignored her.

I nodded concession, gave him a patronizing little clap. 'Okay, Dean. Okay.'

'Okay what?'

'You win.'

'But we're not competing. We're conversing. And in so conversing, if we hold to etymology, we aim not to defeat each other, Mr. Dunn, but to turn one another around. And so, much more than a contest, it is a dance we are in.'

Kendra, who had no patience for this kind of thing, looked at me, then Dean. 'Are you two about done?'

'A person can't be done, Kendra. Only finished.'

She spun around. 'So *are* you?'

'Am I what?'

'Finished.'

'For now.'

'Good.'

'Ah, but there's nothing either good or bad but thinking makes it so.'

She shook her head. 'That's just stupid. Everyone knows what's good and everyone knows what's bad.' Before Dean could respond, she turned to me and said, 'Can we please get back to whatever it is you want us to write down—good or bad—so that we can learn it, recite it, get our ninety, and move on?'

Some of the other students clapped.

'Okay, Kendra. You tell me. Why are Hamlet's final words so perfect, so fitting?'

'I don't know.'

'You don't have to *know*. You just have to have an opinion.'

'I don't have an opinion.'

'That's too bad. You should always have an opinion.'

'Well I don't.'

'Think of his life. What he endures. The chaos. The noise. The disarray. The constant clatter in his head. There is something beautiful in what he says when he comes to the end, don't you think? The quiet revelation, the simplicity of it.'

I noticed two or three students beginning to write. Kendra wasn't one of them. She looked at me.

'You do know he wasn't real, Mr. Dunn.'

'What do you mean?'

'He's made up. Non-fiction.'

'You mean fiction.'

'Whatever the fake one is.'

'Fiction.'

'Sure. Whatever. Who cares?'

I did, for one.

'It doesn't matter how he dies. It doesn't matter how he lives. It's just a story.'

'Kendra, there's no such thing as *just a story*.'

'What does that mean?'

'A good story is much more than words on a page. It shows us what it means to be human.'

'But Hamlet isn't human.'

'Sure he is.'

'No. He isn't.'

'Okay. So what is he?'

'I don't know, but he isn't real, and I don't think we should have to study things that aren't real. It's a waste of time if you ask me.'

'What should we study then?'

'I don't know. History. History happened. People did things. Hamlet didn't do anything. Shakespeare might have. But Hamlet didn't. It's not like he walked the earth. It's not like he was Jesus.'

'I beg to differ.'

Dean said, 'You think Hamlet is Jesus?'

Everyone laughed.

'No, but I do believe Hamlet is resurrected every time someone picks up this play' —I showed them the book— 'and reads his lines.'

Kendra rolled her eyes, shook her head. 'I give up, Mr. Dunn.'

I sighed, but not heavily. 'Again, that's too bad.'

I stood and did the teacher-walk down one row of desks and up another.

'A person should never give up. It's one of the things Hamlet teaches us' —I looked at Kendra— 'whether he was real or not.'

More students started writing.

'Hamlet never relents. Even in his final moments there's no surrender in him, not a whimper. When he realizes he's dying, he asks Horatio to tell his story, and in so doing, conquers death. He understands that a story is the one thing more powerful than the undiscovered country. Nothing can kill a story.'

'Except a bad plot, bad acting, budget cuts.'

This was Dean. He couldn't help himself.

I continued. 'Hamlet persists even when he's gone. We can assume Horatio goes on to tell Hamlet's story because it's in his character—not to mention his name—to fulfill his friend's dying wish. Shakespeare may have written the play, but within the fictional world Horatio is the one who keeps it alive.

'Stories help us remember what it means to be human. And it is a remembering. We all understand what it means to be human, but sometimes we forget.

'And the silence in our stories is *where* we remember, *when* we remember. The perfect irony is that Hamlet remembers only as he takes his final breath. He tells us, as he leaves this world full of sound and fury, *The rest is silence*. In *sleep*, in *music*, in *everything else*—the *rest* is silence. Ultimately, the truth is in what is not said.'

Booker would've been proud. Norman, too.

At the front of the room again I turned and looked at the class, retook my position at the desk, one knee up, shoulders square. And it was then—at that exact moment—that Eckleburg walked in.

Everyone turned. Two policemen stood in the doorway. Avoiding eye contact with me, Eckleburg looked around the room. I stood and folded my arms.

'She's not here today.'

Eckleburg looked at me through her red frames which went with her red shoes. She wore a black suit jacket and black pants. Static emanated from the black walkie-talkie in her hand.

'Who's not here, Mr. Dunn?'

'Chantal.'

'Chantal?'

'Chantal Aster. She's not here.'

It felt strange saying her full name like that. Out loud. In public.

'And why would you think we're here to see Chantal Aster?'

'I don't know. I just assumed—'

The students looked at me, then Eckleburg. Back and forth.

'—so what is it that I can do for you, Mrs. Eckerton?'

'Actually, it's you we need to speak to, Mr. Dunn.'

It was the 'we' that did me in.

The police moved into the room, almost awkward in their uniforms. The vests, the holsters. Black sticks on one side, black guns on the other. Ficticious and real at the same time. Comically threatening.

As though letting someone by, Eckleburg turned her back to the class and extended an arm towards the door. 'If you could please come with me.'

Dean, in a descending, doom-like scale: 'Dunn, Dunn, Dunn.'

Some nervous laughter throughout the room. No one was sure yet whether this was serious. Or how serious. Including me. It felt staged. Like a prank of some sort. Like some candid camera reality show.

'Mr. Dunn. I need you to come with us.'

'I'm not going anywhere until you tell me what's going on.'

She turned to the police. They stepped towards me. One of them leaned in and whispered, 'Mr. Dunn. This is not the place.'

'Yes. It is.'

I was loud. Stupidly loud.

'This *is* the place. Right here. In front of my students. They have a right to know what's going on with their teacher. Besides, I have nothing to hide.'

That was a lie.

'So, either you tell me what you want with me or I'm not budging an inch.'

The policemen checked with Eckleburg. She closed her eyes, nodded once.

Until that moment I had never hit anyone in my life. As the first hand touched my shoulder I pulled away, cocked a fist, screwed my face into a fury, and let fly. To be honest, I can't believe I connected. I'm surprised the one I hit didn't duck or pull some sort of slick defence move. I guess he wasn't expecting a teacher to take a swing at him in front of a roomful of students. He should have known better. I thought it was part of their creed: expect the unexpected.

I've come to pay great heed to this little adage myself.

What can I say? I gave everyone in the room something to talk about. Not that there's any real consolation in it, but I'm certain none of those students will ever forget how their grade twelve English teacher cold-cocked a cop right in front of them.

(*Aside*. What a great phrase: 'Cold-cock.' I could see Hamlet using it. *To raise your fists against a band of troubles and by opposing cold-cock them*. I could see him doing it, too. Early on, when Claudius tries to be all fatherly. Bam! Right in the kisser.)

I looked at my fist. I could still feel the shape of the eye socket on my knuckles. Like an echo. I looked at the body on the floor. Jesus, I thought. I just knocked out a cop.

Everyone looked. Dean in the back had to stand to see. He was beaming, loving it.

And the new, Piss-Ant-Weight Champion of the World, Ben 'What-a-Fucking-Idiot' Dunn!

The other policeman had me off my feet and on the floor before I could even turn and surrender, his knee pressing hard into the back of my head. My nose crushed into the cold hard floor. Eyes watering. Hands behind my back. Zip-tied.

He didn't check with the principal this time. Thwump. Down I went. Just like that. When he pulled me to my feet I could feel the tears coming.

'You have the right to remain—'

'I have the right to remain right here, asshole.'

'—silent. Anything you say—'

'Anything I say? Go fuck yourself. That's what I say.'

I looked at Eckleburg. She was hugging herself, shaking her head.

The policeman continued his speech. 'Do you understand these rights—'

'Understand? Fuck you and your understand. You know nothing of *understand*.'

I was blubbering now. Pathetic. Hard to watch, I'm sure. Hard to listen to. Wet. Whiny. Loud. Impossible to stop. What a mess.

I wanted to wipe my face.

I didn't look at any of the students. It was over. I knew it. Whatever happened, I'd never see them again. Not like this anyway. Not with me as their teacher. Not with me as anyone's teacher.

Eckleburg was at the door, holding it open. She clicked her walkie-talkie. I heard her say Richards' name, then I heard him, his voice through that little black box. At the end of their exchange he actually said, 'Over.'

I hated him.

The policeman I'd hit had a hand on my back. Much nicer than I deserved. 'Let's go.'

I moved towards the door, avoided all eye contact. When I reached Eckleburg I looked at her shoes. Ruby red. Shiny. Like the Wicked Witch of the East.

I spoke to the shoes. 'She told me she was twenty-five.'

That was a lie. She never told me her age. I just assumed. Stupid.

'Who did, Mr. Dunn?'

'Chantal. I didn't even know she was a student. It wasn't my fault.'

Whispers filled the room.

'This is not the place, Mr. Dunn.'

I didn't argue this time.

Richards was outside the door. I knew him from the scuffed brown loafers. He had the walkie-talkie in his hand. I didn't look up. I couldn't.

'Mrs. Eckerton.'

'Mr. Richards. I know this is your prep time, but I was hoping you would look after Mr. Dunn's class until the end of the period.'

'Of course, Mrs. Eckerton.'

I was still looking at the floor. I knew he was grinning. I could tell. I could feel it. The fucker. God, did I hate him.

The policeman's hand on my back again. Through the door. Into the hall. None of the students said anything as I left. Not even Dean.

'What am I going to do now?'

I meant to say this in my head. I was a mess. I wasn't in control of anything. I'm surprised I didn't piss myself, to be honest.

'You should have thought of that, Mr. Dunn, before you decided to traffic marijuana to students.'

I looked up. 'What?'

She hugged herself. It's what she did instead of pocketing her hands or putting them behind her back.

'You heard me, Mr. Dunn.'

She looked at Richards. So did I.

I was wrong. He wasn't grinning. His arms were crossed and he was altogether serious. He didn't say anything. It made me hate him even more.

'Mr. Richards has video evidence that corroborates everything. Plus we have six other testimonies from students who say they made purchases from you.'

Video evidence. Did she just say 'video evidence'? And testimonies? Who the hell would say they bought drugs from me? Kids who had it in for me maybe, kids who'd failed my class. But it wasn't true. How could they believe a bunch of potheads over me? Then I remembered. The night of our last gig, the night I found out about Wyatt, the night I spent with Chantal. Booker and I were waiting outside the bar having a toke when Dean and a couple of his friends walked up. Booker convinced me to give them some of what we had. I know I shouldn't have but I certainly didn't take any money for it. Besides, there's no way Dean said anything. It's not his style.

I shook my head.

Richards standing there all ardent and holier-than-thou. I should have hit him. I don't know why I didn't. What difference would it have made? I should have said, 'Hey, Mr. Richards, you piss-ant,' and then—just as he folded his arms across his chest and went to say something condescending—cold-cocked him. Bam. Right in the kisser.

Eckleburg motioned towards the policeman. I felt his hand in my back again. I started walking, not knowing what I was going to do. I could hear Eckleburg and Richards talking behind me. I hated them. Really, though, what was I going to do?

Booker would say something like: 'Well, Ben Franklin, I wouldn't worry too much about what comes and goes. There's a tendency for things to right themselves. Blue skies are imminent. Survival is a certainty.'

I don't know, Booker. Certainty's a bit of an enigma.

Hamlet would say: 'Come on there, Dunn. Buck up. It's not like you're in prison—yet. Besides, in the grand scheme of things, there's nothing either good or bad but thinking makes it so.'

Oh. Yeah. Right. Good one, Hamlet. Moral relativism. Look where there got me.

This just came to me. This is how it felt. When everything went down the way it did. When Eckleburg came in with her two heavies. When she said everything she said. When I said and did everything I said and did. When Richards affirmed his role as the spur, the splinter under my fingernail. It was like hell itself breathing out contagion all over my world.

That Is the Question

Seven years ago I was a second-year undergrad who had con-vinced himself that it was only a matter of time before The River's Edge was picked up by an indie label and then off we'd go. On the road. Life as musicians. Paid gigs two or three days a week. We wouldn't get rich right away but we'd make enough to live on. Enough to say we made music for a living. Like the Hip in the mid '80s or Sloan and their empty-clubs cross-Canada tour of '92. Like the humble new-millennium beginnings of Great Lakes Swimmers. We'd have one of those touring vans with our name painted on the side. A manager even. Someone like Jimmy Rabbitte, Jr. We'd stay in cheap hotels, sleep till noon, have a beer for breakfast, another for dessert, write a song or two by six, make our way to the bar by seven, sound-check at eight, rock the house from nine till one, pack up, hit the road for the next town, and do it all again. Back then, I couldn't imagine anything better.

In school I was getting through about half the required reading, and understanding about half of that. Not that I aimed to read only half. Not that I didn't try. One thing I can say with certainty is that I've always tried. The problem was it took me a long time to get through the material. Especially the denser stuff like Portrait of the Artist and The Good Soldier. Books like those I had to read twice to make any kind of sense of them. Other books like The Sound and the Fury and To the Lighthouse I was lost on every page. My grades were okay. Nothing stellar. Somewhere just above the average. Never high enough to draw any attention from the profs. I spoke in class when the opportunity arose and at times I think I was able to say some interesting things, but for the most part I was easily missed, forgettable. I was certainly no Dean. I doubt very much any of the profs even knew my name.

Which I was fine with. I wanted to be a musician, not an academic.

But 'want' has very little to do with what you end up with, which is something I haven't learned so much as I've come to know, the way you come to know the words of a song you've heard many times but have never really listened to.

Yet convincing my younger self of eventual success was a surprisingly easy thing to do. Although I had no precedent to go on, and really no clue what success looked like, I was certain that one day I would make a living making music.

I was a dreamer. A believer in 'meant to be.' A romantic. An idealist, Booker called me. But then somewhere along the line all that died and I became a teacher. Then a couple of bad decisions and some bad luck and I became a former teacher. And then what?

Then I went and hid in a country not my own.[10] I had no savings, and so for the couple of months I was there I relied on the money my poor father squirreled away in a tin box under his bed for the last twenty years of his tragically sad and lonely life. A life, as it were, that became little more than a collection of cloned days spent padding the neatly piled bundles of money in said tin box and stupidly waiting for her—the woman he so hopelessly and stupidly loved, the woman who was biologically and in no other way my mother—to return.

'Pathetic.' This is what I said to him the last time I saw him. It was a Sunday in early November. Everything was grey. I'd gone home to Castorville to cook dinner for him and tell him I was leaving for a while. He wouldn't ask where I was going or why and I wouldn't tell him. I wouldn't tell him I was going to find a woman who I'd spent three days with seven years ago and was fairly certain I was in love with. I wouldn't tell him about my forced removal from the school. He wouldn't react anyway. He never did. You could tell him the world was about to end, that there was an hour left for all life on earth, and he'd just sit there, nod, and sip his tea.

The last day I saw him was the day before I left. I went home, like I said, to cook him dinner and tell him I was leaving. I also

---

[10] To look for you. Although at first I didn't even do that.

felt compelled, for some reason I could neither name nor understand, to tell him I loved him, to actually speak the words. I could-
n't remember ever having said them to him in my life. I'm sure I
had when I was young—in those few scant years we were a family, at an age when you say things out of mimicry and repetition—
but I couldn't actually remember saying them. Which is important. A man needs to be able to remember doing certain things.
Not remembering, in the end, isn't much different from not
doing.

When I walked into the house—a place I still held some
vague feelings of 'home' for—with a bag of groceries in one hand
and a six-pack in the other, I found him sitting in the living room,
holding a framed picture of her.

She was beautiful. I will say that. But there was something in
the way she looked at you even from within a photograph that
said she was a woman who loved herself more than anyone else,
a woman who would have no trouble turning her back and walking away from those closest to her. It's strange how when you
know something about a person you can always see it in a photograph, even if at the time of the photograph the thing you
know has not yet happened, even if the person doesn't yet know
it about herself or ever will, even if the photograph was taken in
the days before she had a family and decided one morning to
wake up and walk out on them without notice and never look
back. Like she was an indifferent Orpheus and her family was the
hell she was escaping.

In the years after she was gone I got angry and my father got
sad. The sadder he got, the angrier I got. We grew apart. Until
one day I left too, and I'm not sure he even noticed.

I dumped the grocery bag and the six-pack on the kitchen
table, pulled a can from the plastic ring, and snapped it open. Half
of it was gone before I got to the living room.

I hadn't seen him in two months. He looked up and nodded
hello.

'Thought I'd cook dinner.'

He continued to stare at the TV, gave me another nod. There
was some evangelist show on. A miracle worker. A single touch

of his hand and believers collapsed on the spot. Thousands of brainwashed followers with their eyes closed, hands above their heads, nodding, swaying, muttering, 'Yes, Jesus. Thank you, Jesus. Jesus, Jesus, Jesus,' overcome and instantly healed by the power of the Lord as it came surging through the palm of the waxy-looking man on stage performing miracles. 'Open your eyes and see again! Wipe away the darkness! Hear the Lord, my son! Hear my voice! Say goodbye to the silence forever! Stand and walk! Walk beside your heavenly Father! Wake up! Wake up! Your long lost love is in bed beside you! Look, you're a family again! Praise Jesus! Praise the Lord!'

I finished my can of beer and laughed to myself.

'Where's the converter?'

He gestured towards the coffee table. Not even a hint of a smile.

I flipped through the channels and settled on football. I don't know why. It's not like it was something we shared. I had no memory of a father-and-son Sunday afternoon spent watching the Grey Cup or the Super Bowl. He certainly never taught me how to throw a spiral or cradle a catch on the run.

I do know he played when he was in high school. I remember seeing a picture. A team photo. I can still see him in the back row, near the middle. Number thirty-two. One of the tallest. Tough looking. Cocky. Happy, if I had to guess. Straight, sun-blonde hair swept across his forehead. Thick black lines drawn with a finger under his eyes. Not quite squinting. Arms folded, chest inflated. Elbow-to-elbow with his teammates, his friends. Herculean. Invincible.

How or why I could call upon this picture at will, I do not know. But I could. Whenever I saw something to do with football—an ad, a clip on TV, a pickup game in a field by a school—I always thought of my father. This picture of him. Not the father I knew (not that I knew him at all, really), but the father I might have had. The man that lived in my father's body before he began to fade.

I went to the kitchen and emptied the grocery bag onto the counter: chicken, a box of fries, a container of coleslaw. This was me cooking. I could see the back of my father's head above the armchair he was in. He didn't move. He could've been sleeping. He could've been dead. It didn't matter whether it was people collapsing under the hand of an evangelist or men being tackled on a field—to him, I imagined, it was all the same. People, one after the next and without end, being knocked down.

I brought him some food and a beer. I took the picture from his lap and replaced it with the plate. I was surprised he let me, to be honest. He stared at the TV and ate like a patient in a hospital, forking the food to his mouth with no real purpose or pleasure.

'Beer's good and cold.'

I took a gulp of my own.

'I remembered you like Export.'

The can sat on the table beside him unopened.

He hadn't had a drop to drink since the day she left. When I said I remembered he liked Export it was because, like the football photo, I could summon a picture of him leaning against his first car—an orange 1970 Plymouth 'Cuda—arms and legs crossed, grinning, holding an old stubby bottle of Ex. Like an ad from the '70s.

He nodded.

I tried watching the game. It was slow. Beyond the movement of the ball and the basic idea of getting from one end to the other, I didn't understand any of it. Whistles, yard lines, flags, a field full of men lining up to hit one another every thirty seconds. To be honest, I felt like hitting something myself.

My knee was bouncing. Involuntarily. I didn't really notice. Neither did he. Any normal person would've said something like, 'Hey! Quit the bouncing, will you?'

I looked at him. At the next commercial I got up and snapped open his can of beer. He looked at it and went back to eating.

'Would you just drink the fucking beer.'

He looked at me with no discernable expression.

'Say something. For fucksake.'

He shook his head. That's it. That's all I got. And the worst of it is he didn't mean anything by it. He didn't mean 'no' or 'I'm disappointed' or 'I'm frustrated.' He simply shook his head.

'I don't know why I even come here.'

Then he looked at me and I could see the tears welling. I rolled my eyes, stomped out to the kitchen, dumped my plate in the sink, took another beer, and drank almost all of it at once.

Back in the living room I folded my arms over my chest, beer still in hand. 'This is pathetic. You know that, right? You, me, all of it. Pathetic.'

I wasn't being mean. Not on purpose. I was trying to be honest.

'She's been gone for more than twenty years. Twenty years, Dad. Twenty fucking years and all you do is go to work and sit around this fucking house staring at her picture waiting for her to come back. Newsflash, old man: she ain't coming back.'

I finished my beer and went and got another one. I took his can from the table and forced it into his hand. He looked at it. I hit it with my can and drank.

'You've got to live your life. I mean, really. You have to forget her.'

I took a gulp and burped.

'I know I have.'[11]

Without looking up, he took a sip and nodded. I laughed and slapped his leg.

'There you go, Dad. There you fucking go.'

He rubbed the spot where I hit him. Again I knocked his can with mine. This time it fell into his lap. He let it spill for a second before picking it up. Then he started to cry. Head down, shoulders bobbing, the whole bit.

'Jesus Christ. I can't take it.'

I finished the beer and crushed it underfoot. I knelt in front of him and put my hands on the arms of the chair.

'Look at me Goddamnit.'

He didn't.

'Look at me, will you? Look at me,' I yelled. I was yelling at my father. 'I hate her. You know that? I fucking hate her. I wish she'd walk through that door right now.'

---

[11] That was a lie. Certain things—certain people—you never forget.

I pointed to the front door. He actually wiped his eyes and looked to see if she was there.

'I wish she'd walk through that door so I could tell her right to her face how much I hate her.'

He covered his ears and shook his head. I grabbed his wrists—they felt so small—and pulled away his hands. I was inches from his face.

'I hate her. Do you hear me? I fucking hate her for doing this to us. I hate her for turning you into a pathetic lump of a man. I hate her for leaving me with a father I can't even sit and have a beer with. I hate her for being my mother. I hate her for squeezing me out from between her fucking legs into this shithole of a world. I hate her with every fucking breath I take. I hate her, I hate her, I hate her.'

I let go of his wrists and stood. He covered his ears again even though I was finished. I could hear Big Joe say, 'I ate her,' and I started to laugh. Wickedly. Like Ray Liotta.

I'm sure he questioned how someone so callous could be his son. I'm sure *he* hated *me* at that moment.

Although I never knew my father to pray I pictured him on his knees by his bed, elbows on the mattress, hands pressed together, eyes squeezed shut. 'Oh Lord in heaven. Oh heavenly Father. Please tell me why she left. Give me a reason. Help me to understand. Tell me how a woman can leave her family. And if you can't tell me this, can you at least find her, wherever she is, and tell her I love her? Tell her to come back home so we can be a family again. I don't ask for much, Lord, but I am asking this. She's all I've ever wanted. And now my son hates me for it. He hates me, Lord. My only son hates me.[12] Oh, Lord, please tell me what I've done to deserve all this?'

I pictured Clint Eastwood as God, thundering down his answer. 'Deserve's got nothing to do with it.'

'Tell me, Lord. Tell me what I can do to undo it all.'

'Not a god damn thing, Walter. That's the shame of it. Once something's done you can't undo the doing of it. You can't undo anything.'

---

[12] I didn't though. You need to know that. I loved him. I loved him.

'What about you, Lord? You could undo everything if you wanted to. Oh please, Lord, could you please? Could you please undo it all and put everything back the way it was? Please, Lord. Please?'

From what I can tell, there's no difference between praying and begging.

'I'm sorry, Walter. Sure I am. But nothing can be undone.'

He was right, of course, this Eastwood-God. Which means I can't undo that last afternoon I spent with my father. I can't undo what I said and I can't undo what I didn't say. I can't undo any of it, though I wish I could.

Standing there in front of my weeping father, I shook my head. 'I'm done. I can't do this anymore.'

Again, he didn't say anything.

'I'm leaving. Just so you know.'

As I predicted, he didn't ask where and he didn't ask why.

'I'm going to Ireland. Dun Laoghaire.' Even as I said it, I felt the distance of an ocean between us.

Without a word, he got up from his chair and walked away. I watched him go to his bedroom. He shut the door. Out of habit, I guess, or secrecy, or as a way of saying to me, 'I'm done, too, son. I can't do this anymore either.' It scared me a little.

I stood and took a step towards the room, wanting to tell him I was sorry, not just for that afternoon but for everything. I wanted to thank him. I wanted him to know he'd been a good father. I wanted him to know I loved him. But just as I took that step the bedroom door opened and out he came with the tin box in his hands. He seemed taller all of a sudden, surer of himself, proud.

He held out the box. I took and opened it. It was filled with neatly piled bundles of money. It looked stolen. Like something from a movie. I told him I couldn't and tried to give it back. He shook his head once and I nodded as though I understood something, and tucked the box under an arm.

He put a hand on my back, walked me out, and held the door open as I left. When I got to my car I turned and waved. Such a strange gesture. Sticking your hand in the air at someone. As though you've achieved something. As though you're calling for attention or asking without words to be chosen. *Pick me.* As though you're stretching for something above you. Helpless and drowning, reaching for the air you so desperately need to breathe, as though it undoes everything.

As though. As though.

.　　　.　　　.

My father died two weeks later in his sleep, with no signs of struggle or pain. The cause of death, unknown. He was quiet about everything he did.

I didn't go to the funeral. I'll say I didn't know about it, which is true but still no excuse. I lost my phone the night I got to Dun Laoghaire. I got drunk. For some reason I'd felt like celebrating. What, I don't know. A dozen Guinness later and I barely made my way back to the hotel. When I got there I went to call Booker and couldn't find my phone. There was no way I could retrace my steps. In the morning I barely knew where I was. So—just to confirm—it is my fault I wasn't there. No one could reach me but I'm the one who failed to connect. Somehow I always fail to connect.

It was seven on a Monday morning two weeks to the day after he died that I finally called home. (*Aside.* Strange how we use the word 'home' sometimes.)

'Hello?'

The voice was raspy, heavy with sleep. I should've called Booker. He would've been up.

'Emerson McKnight. Top o' the morning to ya.'

He sighed. I could picture him rubbing his eyes, reaching for the bedside clock. 'Ben?'

'Yup.'

'It's two in the morning, Ben.'

He was trying to whisper.

A female voice in the background, muffled, also heavy with sleep. 'Emerson? Who is it?'

'No one, hon. It's no one. Go back to sleep.'

I was no one.

I could hear the sounds of him getting out of bed, making his way downstairs, flicking on the kitchen light. I could picture where he was exactly. I'd had dinner there a few days before I left. I remember watching in awe as my old bandmate said grace. Out of politeness I went along. Bowed my head, closed my eyes, crossed my chest. The whole hypocritical lot.

Awake now and without whispering, Emerson repeated the time. 'It's two in the morning, Ben.'

'So you said.'

I could hear him sigh.

'I was just having meself a fryup and tea at a wee place called McKnight's and thought, Jesus, Dunn, McKnight's. Imagine that. Got to be a sign from the good Lord above telling you to call your old buddy, Emerson. And I says, sure, it's been too long. Too long. So here I am calling. And now I've woken you up. I feel awful about that. I do. A thousand earnest apologies. And a thousand more to Miss Elizabeth Anne, you'll be sure to tell her.'

'You're drunk.'

'I am so.'

'It must be what, six in the morning there?'

'Seven.'

'How are you drunk at seven in the morning?'

'How'm I drunk at seven in the morning. That's a good question. And I have a good answer. I do.'

He sighed again. At first I thought it was disappointment.

'You're not going to lecture me are you, McKnight? Christ,' I laughed, 'my old man doesn't even do that.'

'Ben?'

'Emerson?' I mimicked him and laughed.

'I don't know how to tell you this.'

'Just let one word fall after the next. That usually works.'

Again, he sighed.

'Jesus, man. Enough with the fucking sighs already.'

He didn't sigh again.

'Come on, man. What is it? Wyatt's gay, you're a Catholic. Let me guess, Booker's a woman. No wait, he's a closeted, teetotalling, Tory literalist. Hah.'

'Ben.'

'Emerson.'

'Your father passed away.'

I didn't hear him right. I couldn't have.

I said nothing. At first I couldn't get my breath. It felt like I was choking.

'It happened two weeks ago. In his sleep. We called all the hotels, but you weren't listed at any of them. We tried, Ben.'

The waitress refilled my tea. I nodded. She smiled. The two men at the table next to me were talking about football. I understood none of what they were saying except that football wasn't football. It was soccer. But when they said the word it didn't matter. *Football.* All I could see was my father in his red jersey. Number thirty-two. In the middle of the back row. Tall. Not quite squinting. Elbow-to-elbow with his friends. He looked happy. Alive. Eternally young.

'Ben?'

I cleared my throat.

'Are you okay?'

Was I okay. That was the question. I nodded, which was a stupid thing to do.

'We tried to find you, Ben. We did.'

'I know. You said.'

'You weren't listed. Not anywhere.'

'No. I know. I wouldn't be.'

'We tried every Byrne that was listed, too. Booker remembered her name.'

'Of course he did.'

I didn't explain and he didn't ask any further.

I said, 'It can't be real.'

'I know.'

No he didn't. How could he?

'The last time I saw him I yelled at him. Did you know that, McKnight? I yelled at my father. I called him pathetic.'

'People say things they don't mean all the time.'

'Yeah, but I'm not people. I'm his son.'

He sighed again. 'The Lord works in mysterious ways.'

Mysterious—a euphemism for nonsensical, unthinking, selfish.

'Bullshit. I called him pathetic. I yelled at my father and called him pathetic. There's nothing Lordy or mysterious about that.'

'I'm sure he knew you didn't mean it.'

'How? How would he know that?'

'I don't know.'

'Exactly. You don't know. Nobody knows. Nobody knows a God damn thing. I took his money too. How do you like that? As though I'd earned it or something. I insulted him and then I took his money.'

'I'm sure he wanted you to have it.'

'Of course he wanted me to have it. For fucksake, McKnight, I didn't steal it.'

'That's not what I—'

'He put a hand on my back when he walked me out. He never did that. It's like he knew and didn't tell me. Jesus fucking Christ, I can still feel his hand on my back.'

'Ben. Please. There's no need—'

I laughed but it wasn't really a laugh. It was short and loud and wicked. I took the phone from my ear, looked at it, and spoke into it like a tape-recorder.

'You're right, McKnight. There's no need. That's exactly what's wrong with the world. There's no fucking need.' Whatever that was supposed to mean.

I set the phone on the table, put my hands in the air like someone who was suddenly saved, looked up, and called out, 'Oh, Lord. Please tell me, Lord. What kind of fucking man am I?'

.   .   .

He was fifty-three years old, my father. Healthy by all accounts. Physically, at least. The autopsy report said he died of natural causes, but there's nothing natural about dying at fifty-three, broken-hearted and alone.

So. I'm alive and in Dun Laoghaire, twenty-six, and on my own. My father is dead.[13] These are the facts. This is what I know, right now. Which is important because what is *now* is really the only thing that can be true. Which essentially means nothing is true since the word 'true' refers to an 'absolute' and there is no such thing as an 'absolute now.' So. Where the fuck does that leave me?

My apologies. I'm high and I'm trying to work through the guilt and figure out what it's all for and what it all means and whether it's worth it,[14] or whether I'm fooling myself writing all this shit down like it means something, like it's worthwhile.

So I'm spewing. What a great word. Spewing. Letting it all flow as it comes. Uncensored, unedited. I'm guessing that's how all the 'How to Write a Book' books say to do it. You know, *just let the words flow from your pen*. Whatever the hell that means. I mean really, no one uses a pen anymore. Besides, you don't learn how to build a house by reading about it. You've got to lose a thumbnail or two. What did Richler say? 'There's only one way to write and that's *well*. The how is up to you.'

This is me figuring out the how.

In the meantime, I wouldn't blame you at all, dear reader, for skipping ahead to the next bit of dialogue. You wouldn't miss a thing. Not really. But if you'll humour me I really do feel compelled to write this little section of hooptedootle. Maybe it's the weed. Who knows. Maybe it's my father's fault. I've already blamed my mother. Why not blame him too.

So. Anyway.

The information in the first two sentences that begin this section are objectively true: I'm alive and in Dun Laoghaire,

---

[13] You are gone.

[14] You know, being here, looking (or not looking) for you.

twenty-six, and alone. My father is dead.[15] The bit about me being high and sad and trying to figure it all out and work through the guilt is also true. The rest of it—everything else I've written up to now (and likely what's to come)—I'm not so sure about. I mean I'm fairly sure, but I'm not unquestionably sure. Fuck, how could I be? I don't have a photographic memory and I didn't record every conversation I've ever had. If that were the case, I would never have done or thought a single thing in my life. In order to be a true and complete observer, you can't be a participant. The opposite is also true. Logically, that is. Not objectively. But the gist—

(*Aside*. There's another great word. *Gist*. I love saying it. *Gist*. And I love what it means: 'the general truth or central meaning of something.' How great is that? How can there be such a thing as 'general truth' when 'truth' itself is by definition 'not general' but 'absolute'? And how can something that is 'generally true,' itself a paradox, also be the 'central meaning,' which, by definition, is also 'absolute'? 'Central' refers to the 'centre,' which is fixed. It is a point. So, in a way, 'gist' refers to the point. Which makes sense, but it also means that the 'gist' should be fixed since it refers to the centre of something. *Gist*. I love the unintentional insidiousness of it.)

—yes, the gist of what I'm writing here is accurate, and by accurate, I mean it is what I believe to be true.

Another problem with truth: belief. When you think about it, there are only two options for any story: true and not true. If the former, in its purest sense, is objective, then so too is the latter, which means intention is irrelevant. Which, by extension, also means it doesn't matter if the author intends to write the truth or not. The funny thing is that words related to the phrase 'not true'—such as dishonesty, deceit, duplicity, and so on—all carry meanings which are fixed to intention. Which means that it does matter whether the author intends to write something that is 'not true' or not. And so, by intending to write something which is not 'not true' the author, logically speaking, ends up writing the truth.

---

[15] And I'm without you.

This is my intention then: to write something which is not 'not true.' So what do we call that, a memoir or a novel? A memel? A novoir? Fiction? Non-fiction? Not fiction? Not non-fiction? Honesty? Too moral. Confession? Too religious. Declaration? Too political. Acknowledgement? Too positive. Admission? Hmn. Admission. Yes, this is what I'm writing.[16]

So.

---

[16] This is what I'm writing, Aislinn. To you. I'm writing an 'admission.' A 'letting in.'

'Ben?'

I opened my eyes but kept my hands in the air above my head. Like Atlas managing the weight.

'Aislinn?'

She was only a few steps away from my table.[17] She stood there, head tilted, smiling, arms folded, a look on her face that said she knew I'd be here, like this had all been arranged, like we'd planned to meet in this little place called McKnight's at seven in the morning on November whatever-it-was, in Dun Laoghaire, Ireland, seven years after spending three days together in Windsor, Ontario.

I thought, This is good. And it was. *She* was. Everything about her. And I don't just mean good. I mean the kind of good that existed before there were any synonyms or hyperboles for 'good.' She was everything that 'bad' wasn't. She was everything that I wasn't. And I knew this as I stood, slightly drunk at seven in the morning, and took her fully in my arms. The sweet silk smell of her hair. The soft, perfect-fit feel of her body against mine. The immediate awareness that the day would pass without us noticing and the morning would come, an Irish sun over the harbour waking us, naked in my rented bed, in my rented apartment, after a night of meant-to-be love seven years in the waiting. Like seven years had been seven days. Like I knew her. Beyond intimacy.

It was like something out of a Hardy novel, meeting her like this. She was alone, in no rush to go anywhere, and free, it seemed, for the day. Perhaps for life. Not to make assumptions or to get ahead of myself, but I couldn't prevent the image from

[17] She is you. Yours is the one name I didn't change. I couldn't. I hope you don't mind.

coming into my head of the two of us being directed by a wedding photographer to look at each other and lean against the granite halfwall of the coal harbour pier on a sun-warmed August afternoon, tourists strolling by, smiling, gesturing to one another to look at the happy couple, Booker and Emerson (maybe even Wyatt) tuxedoed and standing by, my groomed groomsmen chatting with Aislinn's bridesmaids (a sister maybe and a childhood classmate) in their shared role as the people who knew us best, our happy-for-us friends.

Standing there in that little restaurant I didn't want to let her go, but being conscious of this desire to hold on forever I made sure I was the one to initiate the undoing. We came apart like the centre pages of a book being opened, and there we were, laid open to the place we'd left off seven years ago. As though we'd dog-eared time.

'Ben Dunn.'

She wrinkled her nose and shook her head a little.

'Aislinn Byrne.'

So far, all we'd managed to say was each other's names. Twice. The thought crossed my mind that maybe that's all we knew.

'What's it been?'

'A long time.'

She nodded. 'Yes. A long long time.'

We sat at the table. The waitress brought another cup and filled it with tea. She and Aislinn exchanged 'hellos' and called each other by name.[18]

'You look older.'

I touched the back of my head. 'I feel older.'

She sipped her tea. My stomach felt rotten.

'So.'

'So.'

I could hear Chantal saying, *Why do people say 'so' like that? So. It's not what they mean.* But she was wrong. It's not just awkward silence or waiting for someone to speak that makes us utter

---

[18] This was your place in the world, I realized. Your home. I was a just visitor. And an uninvited one at that.

words like *so*. Sometimes our heads and our hearts are so full and there's so much we want to say that it's impossible even to begin. Instead of saying nothing, which is the opposite of what we want to say—because we want to say everything—we say something simple-sounding, and in so doing, we convince ourselves that the other person, the one we want to say everything to, understands.

So.

'Tell me. What brings you all the way over here to the other side of the pond, Ben Dunn.'

She tilted her head. I sipped my tea.

'My father died.'

She leaned forward. 'God. My God, Ben. I'm so sorry.'

I shrugged.

'Was it unexpected?'

I nodded.

'Really, I'm so sorry, Ben.'

I nodded again. There was a pause and she looked at me. Thinkingly.

'You never told me your father was from here. I would've remembered.'

'Oh, no, he wasn't.'

She looked confused.

'I'm sorry. I'm not being very clear.'

She didn't say anything.

'Ask me again.'

'Ask you what?'

'Why I'm here.'

'Okay. Why are you here?'

Her voice had changed: it was guarded, uncertain.

'I heard the fish n' chips were out of this world.'

She nodded, then shook her head.

'Shit. Sorry. It's a glitch. I have a hard time being serious. You probably don't remember that about me.'

She drank her tea and looked over her shoulder. I reached across the table for her hand. Startled, I hoped, or owing simply to reflex, she pulled away.

'If you want to know the truth—'

She looked at me. I couldn't tell what she was thinking.

'—the reason I came over here was to look for you.'

'Really.'

'Absolutely.'

'Well. Here I am.'

She looked over her shoulder again, then at the couple at the table next to us. She made eye contact with them and grinned. The couple was laughing about something.

She turned her cup back and forth by the handle. 'How long have you been here?'

'Couple of days.'

She nodded.[19]

'And how long are you staying?'

'I don't know yet.[20] I bought a one-way ticket.'

Although unromantic and ambiguous, I was hoping my answer would impress her somehow, show her how serious I was, that I had come to begin a life I could commit to, one I could carry through on.

She looked up. 'You know, Ben, I haven't just been sitting by the window pining away. It's been seven years.'

'I know.'

She nodded and looked again at the table, folded a corner of the paper placemat and creased it with her thumbnail. I sipped my tea.

'Pining is such a dramatic word. What about *hanker*? Did you ever *hanker* for me?'

She didn't laugh. Not even a smile.

'You said you'd write.'

'I did write.'[21]

---

[19] You knew I was lying. I could tell.

[20] I should have said something like, 'Forever, if you and the island will have me.'

[21] Another lie. I'd started a few letters but sent none. One night I wrote an email from Booker's computer, but I was drunk and I must've gotten the address wrong. Good thing. I don't remember what I wrote, but I'm sure it was awful.

'You did not.'

'I did. I swear. I wrote every week for a whole year. You never wrote back so I stopped. I figured you'd forgotten about me and moved on. It hurt, if you want to know the truth. I was a wreck.'

'You're lying.'

'I'm not.'[22]

'Fifty-two letters and not a single one makes its way across the sea?'

'I don't know. I must have had the wrong address.'

'They would've been sent back to you.'

'They weren't.'

'Right.'

I shrugged, raised my brow.

'Okay. Let's say you're not lying. Tell me then. When you didn't hear from me, why didn't you call or send an email. How hard would that have been?'

'I hate the phone and I didn't do email back then.'

She rolled her eyes.

'Honest. I didn't even have an account.'

'You had a university account. I found you online and wrote you. At least a dozen times.'

'I only used that account for school, if I had to submit something electronically. Which was almost never. And I had to get help when I did it. I didn't even know how to check what was sent to me. Really. I bet we could go into the account right now and find your messages still there, unopened.'

'Okay then. Let's check.'

She got up and went over to the computers arranged against the far wall. I hesitated, then followed. She sat on a stool and logged in. When she gestured for me to sit on the stool beside her, there was a playful little evil in her smile. Exactly the way she looked at me seven years ago when I went up and sat beside her between sets and told her what a great voice she had.[23] We were at The Coach—a dark, underground Celtic pub

---

[22] I was. Still.

[23] Remember?

that smelled of wood and beer—for our regular Friday night gig. She was sitting at one of the three tables shoved together near the stage. Fifteen Irish girls in soccer jerseys, drinking and laughing and belting out the words to the covers we played.

'Must have been Mary or Jill you heard. They're the singers.'

I grinned. 'No, I think it was you. Your head was back and your eyes were closed.'

'I was only sneezing.'

'Really.'

'I'm allergic to smoke.'

'Hmn.'

'And I don't sing.'

'Well. I think you do.'

'Do you now.'

'I do.'

She took a drink from her pint and nodded. 'So. I'm a liar.'

She sounded serious, pissed off. But I couldn't really tell.

'Well, no, but—'

'So what's it you're saying then?'

I flattened the hair at the back of my head. 'I don't really know.'

'Be a good idea to know what you're saying when you're saying it, don't you think?'

'I guess.'

'You guess.'

'I suppose so.'

'You suppose so. Good. Let's try again. Tell me, what is it you suppose you're saying if you're not saying what you said.'

She had me spinning. I shook my head.

'I thought I knew.'

She ran a hand through her hair and laughed. Not *at* me though.

'See, now you're cute.'

I nodded. 'Now I'm cute.'

'You're all flustered and unsure. Nervous even.'

'And this is good?'

She took another drink.

'I hate it when a guy comes off all full of himself and slick, thinking all he has to do is say the right thing and he'll have you home for a ride that night.'

'Jesus, I didn't mean—'

'Sure you did. You all do. But that's okay. You passed the prick test.'

'The prick test.'

'The metaphorical one anyway. We'll see about the other one later. If you're lucky.'

I'd never met anyone like her.

'I've never met anyone like you.'

'You haven't really met me yet.'

'Right—'

I stuck out my hand. She shook it. Firmly.

'—I'm Ben Dunn.'

'Yes. I managed to get that vital bit of information when you introduced everyone in the band and said, *Thanks for coming. I'm Ben Dunn and we're The River's Edge.*'

'Right.'

She was smiling.

'Can I have my hand back now?'

I let go of her hand and shook my head. 'Sorry.'

'Don't be. Sorry's a terrible thing to be.'

I nodded.

'So.'

'So.'

She took a drink and looked at me like she was waiting for me to say something. When I didn't say anything, she spoke again.

'I'm Aislinn Byrne. You wouldn't know that. As I'm not in the band.'

I nodded. 'No, you're not.'

I nodded again. Differently. Surer this time.

'How would you like to be?'

'How would I like to be what?'

'How would you like to be in the band? Aislinn Byrne.' I mimicked how she'd said her name: *Ashleeng Bairn.*

She laughed. At my pronunciation, maybe, or the invitation, or both.

'There'd be a couple of difficulties with that, Mr. Dunn.'

'Such as?'

'First off, I don't sing. I told you.'

'Yes, you did tell me that. But I don't believe you.'

'Your not believing me doesn't change the truth of it.'

She drank and looked at her friends. They were all talking to one another in little groups.

'So what's the other difficulty? You said there were two.'

'No, I said there were a couple.'

'Yes. A couple. Two.'

'Not every couple is two.'

'Fair enough. But now you're just stalling.'

'Well, Mr. Dunn, my accent's real, in case you were wondering, which may tell you I'm not from here.'

'I had an inkling.'

'Sure, you're the quick one.'

'Nothing gets by me.'

'You're certain about that now.'

'I am.'

She grinned, touched my arm. 'I bet I could get by you.'

I read the name on her soccer jersey out loud. 'Dun Laoghaire Dallyers.'

She sensed my confusion. 'It's ironic.'

'What is?'

'The name. And that you missed it. You know, being the one who lets nothing by him and all.'

I nodded. 'I didn't miss it.'

'Course not.'

She waited.

'And what about where I'm from? Sure, you didn't miss that either.'

I looked at her.

'See, that's the other difficulty, Mr. Dunn. Where I'm from's more than three thousand miles away. Might make getting to rehearsals and gigs a bit of a task.'

'That's true. But it might be to our advantage. We've been talking about going on tour in England. All the serious bands do it. You could be our in.'

She slapped my shoulder and smiled. 'What fucking England? I'm from Ireland, you.'

Across the table, her friends were laughing. The bar was loud. You had to lean in to hear the person next to you. Aislinn and I had been leaning in the whole time. Her skin smelled of summer. Like the sun.

She raised her pint to her friends. They raised theirs in return. Everyone drank. They all broke into song, even Aislinn. After a verse she leaned in even closer. Her mouth at my ear. I could feel her breath. She was whispering. My heart thumped. I couldn't understand what she said. I asked her to repeat it. She got even closer. Her lips touched my ear.

'I'm just drunk enough.'

She squeezed my leg, kissed my cheek, and laughed. I was a little scared, to be honest.

'You know, to sing.'

'Sing. Right. Sing.'

'What'd you think I meant?'

'I knew what you meant.'

Her hand was still on my leg. She squeezed. 'I know what you hoped I meant.'

'No.'

'Yes.'

I felt like an idiot.

She asked me if I knew Eileen Aroon.

I grinned. 'Not personally. But I bet she's lovely.'

'The flower of the hazel glade.'

'Like you.'

She made a retching sound.

'Sorry.'

'Ah, now, you've forgotten already what I said about being sorry.'

'Right. Sorry. I mean—okay, starting now, I'll be the opposite of sorry—just one thing, what's the opposite of sorry?'

She smiled. 'Happy.'

'Okay then. That's what I'll be.'

     .   .   .

I clicked the mouse and struck the Enter key three times hard.

'Here' —she laughed a little— 'you'll break it. Let me do it.'

We switched stools.

Click. Click. Click.

'Okay. Username.'

'Show-off.'

'That sounds about right.'

'Funny.'

'Seriously. Do you know it?'

'The only one I can ever remember using is *Been Done*.'

'Cute.'

She typed.

'Password?'

'I don't know if it'll work.'

'We'll try it. What is it?'

'It won't work.'

'Just tell me.'

I touched the back of my head. 'Eileen Aroon.'

She smiled without looking at me, typed the name, and hit enter.

'The password you have entered is incorrect.' She was reading off the screen.

'I don't know what it is then.'

'I don't believe you.'

'Why would I lie?'

'Because you don't want me to get in.'

'I do want you to get in. Believe me. Try The River's Edge.'

She did. I watched her and it didn't work.

'You forgot the apostrophe.'

'You can't use apostrophes in passwords.'

'Why not?'

'You just can't.'

'Well, that's stupid.'

She shrugged.

'Humour me. Can you try it?'

She did.

'Invalid key. See? Told you.'

'Since when is an apostrophe invalid? No wonder the language is in the state it's in.'

'You're stalling.'

'I'm not.'

I really wasn't.

I thought for a minute and then it came to me, like a slap in the face. I closed my eyes and sighed, defeated by the achievement of this particular remembering. Defeated because of who the remembering made me think of. Password suggestions always include your mother's maiden name. I didn't know her maiden name, but I knew where she came from. I remember thinking that the purpose of a password is to keep people out, an idea which suited my feelings for her perfectly. So I used the only thing I could think of that made me think of her. The place, in the end, she left us for.

I nodded once and spoke to the wall in front of me. 'The password is Fredericton.'

She typed it and it worked.

'We're in.'

I could sense her scanning the screen.

Above the computer was a framed print of an abandoned barn. I stared at it. It looked real. Like a photograph. Most of the red paint on the barn was faded or peeled off. Sections of barnboard were missing. The roof was sagging. The remnants of a season's crop of hay spilled from the barn's loft window and lay strewn on the ground. An old dog, camouflaged by the colours around it, lay asleep by the rusted plough which sat beside the barn, the abandonment of the place reaffirmed by the tall grass climbing up the rusted frame of the plough. There were no other signs of life anywhere. The sky was grey and without the sun.

There were other standard looking prints placed above each of the computers. A boat in a storm, an empty lounge chair on a dock, an old Underwood on a desk in a book-lined room, a sheet of paper spilling from the top, the desk chair pulled out, light spilling through the window, curtains ruffled by imagined wind.

I spoke without fully realizing it. 'Ben Frederick Dunn.' I'd almost never had occasion to write my full name or say it out loud.

I said it again, 'Ben Frederick Dunn.'

Aislinn tapped my shoulder, waved her hand in front of my face. 'Earth to Ben.'

I turned to her. 'I just realized.'

'What—your own name?'

I nodded.

'Well, we all have our little epiphanies, I suppose.'

'You don't understand.'

'Enlighten me.'

'My middle name is Frederick.'

She nodded. 'I caught that. It is remarkable, yes.'

'My last name is Dunn.'

'Another one for the ages.'

'Say them together. Quickly.'

She did and nodded again. 'I get it. Very clever.'

'No. You still don't understand.'

She waited.

'That's where she's from.'

'Who—that's where who's from?'

'My father's one-time wife.'

'You mean your mother.'

I shook my head, nodded.

'Okay. And?'

'Don't you see what this means?'

She shook her head.

I squeezed my right hand into a fist—squeezed and squeezed—then opened it and watched the blood return.

'It means *she* named me.'

In the three days we spent together seven years ago Aislinn and I never got into our personal histories. There had been no point. At the time, the present was all that mattered.

I looked at the picture of the barn and asked her what she saw.

'I'm not much of an art interpreter.'

'I mean what do you see, in there.' I pointed at the computer.

'Turns out you weren't lying this time. They're all here. Every email I sent. Unopened.'

She ran a hand through her hair.

'I'm going to delete them.'

She wasn't asking. I watched her move the cursor over the screen. *Click. Click. Click.*

People who knew how to recover such things would be able to, if something really important depended on it. But what was to be between Aislinn and me, if anything, did not depend on what was composed in a series of emails written seven years ago. What she had written then didn't matter now. (*Aside.* Strange how something can matter so much in one moment and so little in the next.)

'Sometimes it's better not to know, if you're given the option to choose.'

I nodded. 'You're right. Knowing is overrated.'

She looked at her watch.

I said, 'You have to go.'

'Yes. I should.'

I nodded again. 'Well, I'm glad I found you.'

'Technically you didn't. Find me, I mean. You have to be looking for the thing in order to find it. Otherwise it's just happenstance.'

'Happenstance.'

'Yes. We happened upon one another. By chance.'

'Well, then. I'm happy for this happening.'

She touched my arm. 'Me too.'

Standing, she pulled a business card from her back pocket and handed it to me. 'This is my shop.'

The card read:

B.U.T.

BYRNE'S UNIQUE TOUCH

60 UPPER GEORGE'S STREET

DUN LAOGHAIRE DUBLIN

4—BEAUTY

WWW.BYRNESUNIQUETOUCH.COM

There were no pictures or little icons on the card indicating what type of shop it was.

'What exactly do you sell?'

She pointed at the name on the card. I said I didn't get it.

'Say the letters together. Quickly.'

I did. Out loud.

'So that's what I sell.'

I nodded. 'Clever—but the letters actually spell *but*. Doesn't that confuse people?'

'They also spell the French *but*, which fits perfectly.'

'Boo?'

'As in, *Mon but dans la vie est . . .*'

I shrugged, shook my head.

'You don't speak French.'

'No.'

'But you're Canadian.'

'Yes.'

'I thought you were the culturally enlightened half of the continent.'

'We advertise well.'

'Isn't it mandatory in school?'

'Enlightenment? It varies.'

She laughed. 'No. French.'

I shrugged. 'To a point, I guess. But the kind of French you take in school makes you an expert in the subtle differences between *-er* and *-ir* verbs. And that's about it. Almost no one can speak it by the end.'

'That's a shame.'

'Now there's something I'm familiar with.'

She tilted her head, gave me a sympathetic frown.

I said, 'So what does it mean?'

'What does what mean?'

'The French thing you said.'

'My aim or purpose in life is . . .'

I waited. She looked at her watch again.

'You have to go.'

She nodded. 'It was really nice bumping into you like this, Ben.'

'Yes. It was.'

She turned on a heel and I watched her leave. I went back to my table and drank the rest of my tea. It was cold and strong. Like medicine. My head felt weird and my guts were rotted. I felt like Jimmy Rabbitte, Sr. the morning after he and Bimbo went out on the town in their suits on the hunt. I was full of the guilt too, but it was different from the kind of guilt a man gets from the pint. It was deep and hidden and it gnawed at me, and I realized it had been like this for a long time. If you want to know the truth.

.   .   .

Later that night, I wrote a letter (the pen and paper kind) and sent it to Booker. Here's what I wrote:

Hey Booker,

I was thinking. Happenstance is an event that might have been arranged but was really accidental. Nothing planned, no intention. A happening plus a circumstance—not chance.

There's no chance in circumstance. The 'happening' is easy to identify. The 'happening' is the event itself. Like Aislinn and I bumping into one another in a café this morning. But what about the circumstance(s), the environmental condition(s) which affect the event?

Really, circumstances are endless because every event is affected by that which precedes it, ad infinitum. But in practical terms, you can identify the major circumstances for any one event by isolating the event itself within the temporal limits of beginningpoint A and endpoint B. For example, beginningpoint A: Aislinn walks into a café in Dun Laoghaire and sees me with my hands in the air and says my name. Endpoint B: she turns on her heel and leaves. The circumstances for said event, as I see them, are as follows. One, I was still slightly drunk. Two, I'd just found out my father had died. Three, we were in a place which, for the most part, was foreign to me and home to her. Four, she had witnessed me calling out to a God I don't believe in. And five, it had been seven years since we'd seen each other. There was nothing accidental about any of these circumstances. So if the event itself is the only accidental part of happenstance, then it must be the circumstances which give an event its meaning and not the event itself. The question is, considering the circumstances listed above, what did it mean bumping into Aislinn the way I did?

Ben

I had his response in little over a week. Which is pretty quick when you think about it. And really, what's a week? Weeks come and go almost without notice. My father had nearly three thousand of them in his life. If you had three thousand dollars in your pocket, what would a single dollar be? Almost nothing. So a week, in the grand scheme of things, is virtually instantaneous. Not like email, of course, or a text or Facebook or snapchat or any of the rest of it, but still, I'd like to see the oldfashioned type of correspondence make a comeback. The thing about modern messages is there's no sense of purpose. The act of the message itself becomes the reason. Which is wrongheaded. The other thing is, reason goes out the window. If you send someone a message at nine in the morning and you don't hear back from him by noon, you lose all sense of social protocol. *Why hasn't he responded—It's been three hours—He must be upset—I must have offended him somehow—Maybe what I wrote had the wrong tone—Did I use allcaps anywhere?—I'll check my sent-box—Shit, I did use allcaps, but I meant it as a joke—He must know that—He's not stupid—Anyway, who's he to be upset?—I'm the one who should be pissed off—Who does he think he is?—Too important, too busy to send a ten-second email—I know he checks his messages every ten minutes—Well, you know what, fuck him—Fuck him!—That's the last time I send him anything—Good riddance you self-important prick bastard—I should write that and send it—I should—I'm going to—I need to assert myself more—*Click 'Open'*—*Click 'Compose'*—Dear fuckwad, Just a quick message to say good riddance, you self-important prick bastard—*Click 'Send.'*

What's more, handwritten letters are real. They're physical. Impressions in paper. Fold lines. Smudge marks. The smell of ink. The crinkle in your hands. This I know: the only way to make thoughts real is to marry the cerebral to the physical. Like in a book. Otherwise, all you have is thought, and we all know that thought in isolation is the forerunner of insanity and fear. From the Prince himself: conscience does make cowards of us all. Yes sir, it does. Especially when resolution gets all fucked up with the pale cast of thought.

I'll tell you this: one thing I don't want to be is a coward.

.　　　.　　　.

Here's what Booker wrote in his return letter. As only Booker can.

(Hey) Ben Franklin,

What kind of word is 'hey' anyway? It sounds like an unfinished 'hail' which is pretty regal and nearly opposite in tone to that which is intended by 'hey' and too close to the German 'Heil' if you ask me. Also, a homophone to 'hay' which sounds, when put in front of someone's name, almost like you're poking fun at the person's rural roots. And it's often said quickly without the breathless 'H' at the beginning which makes it sound an awful lot like the interjection 'eh' which we use to express any number of meanings and emotions depending on the context, as in 'Eh, get off my lawn you little shit' or 'You know you're not allowed to deface public property like that, eh?' or just simply 'Eh?' And then there's the whole written versus oral communication conundrum. Which is my central point. People say 'hey' when they see one another. I can't see you when I'm writing this, so why would I write/say 'Hey' or 'Hello' or 'What's up?' (a phrase which has an entirely different set of problems all its own) or any other expression of greeting? In fact, I don't for the life of me know why people begin letters with anything other than the actual beginning of the message they intend to impart. If the envelope is addressed to me, then I know the contents must be intended for my eyes. So why write my name at the top of the letter? What I'm getting at, Ben Franklin—and please note the irony—is one should always aim to be economical with one's words when writing. And if one really wants to say 'Hey' then one should pick up the phone, dial the number, and say, 'Hey.'

Now, to the meat of your letter. There are three questions you pose. The first, almost certainly, is rhetorical. The last, without doubt, is posed to me, the reader, and the middle one might be taken either way.

To the last first: 'What do you think?' where 'you' is 'me,' Booker.

Answer: I think any number of things, as everyone does, governed mainly by, but not limited to, these three factors: one, the time of day it is and subsequently what I'm most typically doing at said time-of-day and whether I'm actually doing the typical thing or not, and if I am why I am, and if I'm not why I'm not. Two, the most recent thing I experienced which was unexpected, unplanned, or out of my control (such as receiving a letter in the mail from a friend, getting laid, or missing the bus). And three, the last substantial piece of writing I spent any amount of time reading (mostly fiction or philosophy, although sometimes the side of a cereal box warrants a little contemplative reflection, as does a letter I receive, like yours to me).

To the first: 'But what about the circumstance(s), the environmental condition(s) which affect the event?'

Your parenthetical pluralization, although thoughtful and bases-covering, is unnecessarily inclusive and worse, inaccurate. There is no such thing as a single 'circumstance.' Nor is there ever only one condition (in the context, that is, of 'environmental conditions' affecting an event). Next, the interrogative phrase 'what about' suggests two questions, best illustrated by examples rather than definitions: one, 'what about this question don't you understand? (id est, what don't you understand about this question?). And two, 'what about dinner?' (id est, would you like to have some—or perhaps 'go to' depending on the asker's relationship to the askee—dinner?). And so, even though context usually clarifies the intent, the question 'what about' is an example of ambiguous diction. Instead you should ask 'How do the circumstances (the environmental conditions) affect the event?' To this, considering the five circumstances noted in your letter, I write . . .

Anyone witnessing another human being calling out to God beyond the walls of an established God-calling arena must know that the God-caller has recently, or is currently, or is about to experience one of three scenarios: one, a life-altering event (such as the loss of someone significant in the God-caller's life, as in your case); two, pain, either physical or mental; or three, an orgasm induced by a secondary party. Unless the God-caller is an habitual, many-times-a-day God-caller, and in that case there is no explaining it. Or the God-caller is drunk, which explains everything.

To answer the question more directly, the most significant of the circumstances you list, Ben Franklin, considering the event itself, are these: you were in a place which was foreign to you and home to the woman you claim to love and had not seen for seven years. Time and place is what everything comes down to.

To the middle question whose answer, perhaps, holds the most influence: 'Considering the circumstances, what did it mean bumping into Aislinn the way I did?'

As you likely can guess, I cannot (more importantly, I will not) venture an effort to know or articulate any level of meaning which does not directly involve me. Meaning with respect to anything disconnected from the self is unattainable. In fact (and there are very few such facts to be in), it does not exist.

I hope you find yours.

Booker

Post Script. Consider hopping the Channel in December. Exams and papers will be finished. We'll get drunk up and down George St. If she's willing, bring Aislinn. I know not wanting to leave her (assuming you have indeed found her and your letter to me was not hypothetical) is the only reason you wouldn't come.

What Should a Man Do

Part I

'How do I catch him, Booker?'

'Who?'

'Richards. That piss-ant.'

'Your filmmaker friend.'

I nodded.

'How do you catch him doing what?'

'I don't know. Something. I want to make him pay. The fucker.'

It was catching up with me, how he'd had me fired and run me out of town the way he did. I needed to do something. What kind of man would I be if I didn't?

Booker shrugged. 'Make a film of your own.'

'How? He's as straight as they come.'

'Set a trap.'

'A trap.'

'You know, write yourself a little play. Like Hamlet.'

'I wouldn't know where to begin. I've got nothing on him.'

'He didn't have anything on you either.'

'He thought he did. He thought I was selling dope to students.'

'But you weren't.'

'No. But he made it look like I was.'

Booker nodded. 'Because he believed it.'

'So whatever I do I have to believe it.'

'It'll help. Belief is a powerful weapon.'

I made a fist and hit the table. He shook his head.

'Anger is an impediment though. It muddles things. Convince yourself of something negative about him. I'm sure you can do that. Indeed, I'm sure you already have. Man convinces himself of things all the time without evidence. It's one of our greatest powers.'

I leaned in. 'Okay, say I think of something. Like he's filming girls in the change room or skimming money from those stupid little book sales he runs. How do I catch him doing something he's not doing?'

'That's what the trap is for.'

'Right—but how do I lure him in?'

'You'll think of something. Every man has his cheese.'

I folded my arms and leaned back in the chair. Booker finished his pint and went to the bar for another round. We were in the Rose & Thistle on Water Street. Ron Hynes was just about to take the stage. It was the middle of December in St. John's. The night was young but already bloodthickly black and bone cold. Not for the feint of heart. Not for the sober of spirit.

When he returned, Booker stood the pints on the table and lowered himself into his chair. Crossing his legs, he spoke to the ceiling with an affected poet's voice. Solemn, comical, and musical all at once. As if Dylan Thomas were doing an impression of himself on Saturday Night Live.

He raised his glass. 'Oh, ho, ho, but on the humdrum wrongs of men does sweet vengeance await.'

Aislinn didn't come with me to St. John's. I never got a chance to ask her.[24]

It was late in the afternoon the day after I got Booker's letter in the mail that I went to her shop on Upper George's Street. (I'd been drunk again the night before and on into the morning, and so I'd slept away most of the day.) It really wasn't far at all from where I'd been staying. So close, in fact, that it struck me as odd we hadn't run into each other sooner. Anyway, there I was, standing in front of her shop with no idea what I was going to say. I hadn't thought that far ahead.

The front of the shop was all glass but tinted so you couldn't see in. The name was embossed in the same stylish type as the business card she'd given me. Again, no icons or images. The U in the name was wine coloured. Every other letter was white.

I don't know how long I stood there. I'm sure I looked lost. Scared even. It felt a little like being in a lineup, unable to see the eyes of the accusing on the other side of the glass.

I was wearing the jeans I'd slept in, a hoodie, and a toque. I hadn't shaved in a week. I wasn't thinking about how I looked, to be honest. I stood there running over what I might say when I walked in and saw her in the midst of doing whatever it was she did behind this tinted glass, within her shop, within her life.

The door opened and she stood there, leaning against it, hugging herself against the cold.

'Sorry, sir, but we have a strict no loitering policy.'

My heart quickened. 'I wasn't loitering. I was lingering.'

'There's a difference?'

---

[24] Really, that's why I ran after you the way I did that night outside your shop. I wanted to ask you to come with me. To give us a chance. I don't know why I grabbed you the way I did. I don't know why I said the things I said. If only I could undo it all. I wish I could. I really do.

'Yes, well, one means to remain somewhere for no obvious reason. The other, to be slow in parting or slow to act.'

I wish I could stifle myself sometimes.

'And which pertains to you?'

'I like to think I'm not without reason.'

'So you're slow to act.'

'Notoriously.'

She smiled and rubbed her bare arms, turned and went in. I caught the door and followed her.

Everything inside was shades of white and wine. The checkered ceramic floor, the cash register, the armchairs in the waiting area, the four leather barber's chairs, the comb jars on the counters, the combs themselves, the bottles of product on the shelves, the flowers in the corners, the maxims on the walls, brushed on by a perfect cursive hand: Beauty is a form of genius; It is better to be beautiful than to be good; Beauty is the wonder of wonders. Beneath each line an em-dash and the initials O.W.

Aislinn folded her arms. 'So. What do you think?'

I walked around like a building inspector, nodding stupidly, hands shoved in my pockets. I scratched my head through my toque, looked at the ceiling. 'It's nice. Very Irish.'

I felt the other stylist turn her head. Aislinn told me *very Irish* wasn't exactly what they were going for.

'No—I mean—you know, the sayings on the wall. They're a nice touch.'

I felt like an idiot. Standing in the middle of this beautiful place beside this beautiful woman. One stupid thing after another spewing from my stupid mouth.

Aislinn smiled and touched my arm. The blood rushed to my face. I scratched my head and looked at my feet. She took me to one of the empty barber's chairs, directed me into it with her hands on my shoulders, draped a chair cloth over me and fastened it around my neck. Looking at me in the mirror, she plucked the toque from my head and tussled my hair. Snipped the air with her scissors.

Snip snip.

She put her mouth to my ear and whispered. 'Tell me the truth. Now that I've got you in my chair. You never wrote me. Did you. Not even once.'

I looked at her in the mirror. She was close enough I could smell her hair. I shook my head.

'I didn't think so. It's alright. I haven't been completely honest with you either.'

I didn't ask her what she meant. At the time, I didn't want to know.

Standing behind me, she sifted my hair through her fingers and spoke to the room. 'What are we going to do with you?'

I shrugged. 'Whatever you want.'

She snipped the air again. 'Did you hear that, Annie? Whatever we want.'

Annie was styling another woman's hair. 'We haven't had anyone in the back in a while.'

'Sure, but doesn't he look like he could use a little of what's in the back.'

'Sure he does.'

'I'll clean him up first.'

Aislinn began snipping away. I asked what was in the back and Annie spoke without looking at me.

'Seen Pulp Fiction?'

I grinned, nodded. 'She's funny.'

Aislinn used her fingers to still my head. I felt the cold scissors against my temple.

'Hold still. I'd hate to nick you.'

Annie said, 'Blood stains are hell to get out.'

'It was Annie's idea for the colour.'

'Easier to cover up our little mishaps.'

She smiled. Devilishly.

'Good thinking. I have to say, though, it looks more like wine than blood to me.'

'Blood, wine. We're all Catholics here.'

'Not all of us.'

Annie smiled. 'Sinner. What are you then?'

What was I. That was the question.

'I don't know. Agnostic.'

'Sounds painful.'

I shrugged. 'You get used to it. It's fairly comfortable as far as fences go.'

Aislinn put her hands on my shoulders. 'Hold still.'

'Sorry.'

Annie said, 'Least you're not Protestant.'

I watched Aislinn in the mirror as Annie and I bantered back and forth. She was smiling, sort of, but I couldn't tell whether she was listening to us or if her mind were elsewhere.

Annie undid the chair cloth from her customer's neck, peeled it off, and flapped it once like a bullfighter. The woman in the chair turned her head from one side to the next, checking herself in the mirror.

'Annie, you're a genius.'

'Ah, you make it easy, Flo.'

Flo was probably fifty-five or sixty, but she was doing everything she could to confuse her audience into thinking she was not yet forty. At quick glance, she was succeeding. Standing at the till, she waved off her change and told Annie to keep it.

'You'll have the lowest of the low in here. You should be charging double.'

She handed Annie more money.

'It's Linn. I told her, but she's all about serving the common man' —she gestured at me— 'as you can tell.'

'Aislinn, dear. For the love of God's son, raise your prices. You'll put yourself and poor little Reilly on the streets if you keep this up.'

Aislinn glanced at me in the mirror. The look on my face was ambiguous at best, which took some effort. I'd already noticed the school photo of the boy tucked in the corner of the mirror. I tried to convince myself it was a nephew or Annie's son or someone else's regular work station altogether. But I knew as soon as I saw his six-year-old face looking back at me. The eyes, the black silk hair. He was her son. There was no doubt. And the pensively mischievous look he had, the way one corner of his mouth went up a little higher when he smiled. I knew as soon as I saw him. I knew.

Annie responded quickly, knowing, I can only assume, that Aislinn would have preferred to have been the one to tell me about Reilly. If at all.

'Be better if he *were* in the streets, that one. More natural. Linn has him set up like a real person in that wee apartment of hers. Eats right off the table. Sleeps in her bed. Has the life of himself, sure he does. I told her she needs to get out and find herself a man, but then she goes and drags the likes of this one in.'

It was a good cover. She was quick. If only there hadn't been the picture.

I couldn't see Flo's face from where I was sitting, but I'm sure her expression was one of befuddlement. Confused as she was, and perhaps catching on to Annie's lead, she said nothing more about Reilly.

'See you next Tuesday, Flo.'

'My Jesus. The language on you, Annie. Filthy.'

'I thought you said I was a genius.'

Flo opened the door to leave. 'Genius, yes—well mannered, no.'

'Ah, Flo. Don't go away mad now.'

'I'm not a dog, Annie.'

'Right. Angry then. Don't go away angry. It's unbecoming.'

'Sure, if anyone knew what it meant to be coming.'

Aislinn bit her bottom lip. I raised my brow. Annie let out a laugh like she'd been hit in the stomach.

'Flo. You are a card, love.'

'The Queen of Hearts, my dear.'

I heard the bell go off again. Annie returned to her station, fixed her hair in the mirror.

'How you haven't driven us out of business I don't know.'

'I'm a genius. Didn't you hear?'

'You're mad enough.'

'You worry too much, Linn.'

Annie grinned, took the wine coloured mug from her counter. (Or blood-coloured, depending on your perspective.) 'Tea?'

Aislinn nodded. I took the offer to be for both of us and said, 'Yes. Please.'

Annie looked at me in the mirror. 'Awful polite for a bum.'

There was an edge to her voice suddenly that was less banter and more insult. Maybe the edge had been there from the start and I'd missed it.

She left and Aislinn and I said nothing while she was gone. I didn't know what to say. Neither did she.[25]

Annie returned in a few minutes with three cups of tea. She set Aislinn's on the counter and I watched the steam rise from it. I freed my hands from beneath the chair cloth and took mine.

'Thank you. I appreciate it. Really.'

Annie raised her brow and took a sip of her own tea. 'Sure, you're full of the guilt you are.'

I furrowed my brow. 'Why would you say that?'

'I'm sure you know.'

'I'm sure I don't.'

Annie looked at Aislinn who shook her head, almost unnoticeably. 'Overblown politeness is a sure sign of guilt.'

It went quiet again. Only the *snip snip* of the scissors and the individual sips of tea. When Annie was finished her cup, she set it on the counter and grabbed her bag, said she was on her way. She touched Aislinn's arm, kissed her on the cheek.

'You're okay?'

Aislinn nodded.

'We'll see you tomorrow then.'

I thanked her again for the tea and told her it was a pleasure meeting her. She looked at me as if to warn me and left.

Soon after, Aislinn undid the chair cloth from my neck. 'Annie can be tough to talk to.'

I ran a hand through my hair. 'I don't know what I did.'

'You didn't do anything. She's just looking out for me.'

I nodded. 'She's a good friend then.'

'She is.'

'Can I ask you something?'

She hesitated. I saw her glance at Reilly's picture. She nodded yes.

---

[25] Or I'm sure you would've said it.

'What is it she's looking out for exactly?'

She shrugged. 'Annie knows a lot about me.'

'I see.'

'I don't know that you do.'

I nodded again.

She busied herself putting things away, tidying the counter. It was well after five but I didn't want to leave. I wanted to tell her she was why I was here. I wanted to tell her she was the only reason I was here at all.

I drew a hand over the week's growth on my face. 'I've always wondered what a straight shave would feel like.'

She smiled. 'You trust me with a blade at your neck?'

'It'll be—'

'What, erotic?'

'No.'

'Don't lie.'

'It'll make me feel—I don't know—like a new man.'

'Like a new man.'

She draped the chair cloth over me again, fastened it around my neck.

'That would be a start.'

She thwopped the razor against the leather strap, took a soap brush and bowl, and lathered my face. Standing behind me, she pulled my head into her body. Set her face close to mine. The blade to my neck. She told me to relax. I closed my eyes and waited for the stroke.

The sound was what I expected—like paper ripping, only deeper—but the feeling of the blade moving across my skin was almost undetectable. As though she were using a finger to wipe the lather away. Gentle. Careful. Precise.

The whole process took only a few minutes. When she was finished I opened my eyes. Standing in front of me she took my face in her hands with a warm wet cloth and patted my skin. She stood back and admired her work.

I touched my face. She folded her arms.

'Almost too clean. I'm not sure it suits you.'

She handed me my toque. I put it on.

'What do you think?'

'You were right. Like a new man.'

She busied herself tidying the counter again, sweeping the floor around the chair. I watched her.

'So. Are you going to tell me?'

She continued sweeping and didn't look at me. 'Tell you what?'

'You know[26]—about what's in the back.'

She set the broom against the wall and smiled. 'The tanning bed.'

I nodded. 'Guess I could use a little colour.'

'You're a shade away from a vampire, you are.'

'Come on. I'm not that bad.'

'You're bad enough.'

She looked at me. Her voice changed.

'Which *should* keep me away.'

I was still sitting. Facing me, she climbed into the barber's chair. Slipped one knee in beside me, then the next. Took my face in her hands. Kissed me. I held her waist, slipped my hands under her shirt. She whimpered. I kissed her harder and she began to move herself against me. When I stood, she held on. Hands on my neck, legs wrapped around me, mouth pressed against mine. She weighed almost nothing. I set her on the counter, worked her jeans to the floor. She took my bottom lip in her teeth, undid my belt, freed me, took me in her hand, guided me in. I pushed and she bit down on my lip. The pain went with the heat and we fucked like it was the end of the world, surrounded by all the confusions of love and eternity. We came together, eyes squeezed shut, mouths wide open. Our bodies shuddered like a string plucked with a thumb. The lingering hum of it. The two of us, fading at all our ends.

---

[26] Who Reilly was.

We were eight or nine pints deep. Maybe ten. I'd lost count. Hynes was into his third set. He'd just played 'From Dublin With Love' and 'What if I Stayed.' I'd been singing along. Not so loud that anyone could hear me, except maybe Booker. But he was working on a couple of undergrads who'd come in earlier and recognized him as their Existentialism TA. He certainly wasn't paying any attention to me. Not that I blame him for what happened, but if we'd been alone at the table I know he would have reached out and grabbed me as I rose, self-important finger in the air. He would have said something pointed and jarring. It would have been enough to stop me, make me nod, smile, and sit back down. It would have saved me the embarrassment. I would have ended the night an hour later, singing down George Street, an arm about Booker's neck, his about mine, our polluted breath puffs of white in the cold dark December night. I would have fallen asleep on my friend's couch, unfinished beer and half-eaten pizza on the coffee table, and I would have woken with the typically minor regrets and heavy head of a gut-rotting, sodden night of suds and song.

But we weren't alone and he didn't stop me.

The opening chords of 'My Old Man' rang out from Hynes' guitar and he began to sing. I leaned back, clasped my hands behind my head, closed my eyes, and nodded to the rhythm.

'Sometimes I feel just like him, feel like I'm standing in his shoes, in the very ones he would use, on the watery decks on the Atlantic sea.'

(*Aside*. My father never stepped foot on a watery deck on the Atlantic sea. Not as far as I know. Then again, maybe he did. I hadn't known my father the way I wish I had. But like the song says, I do feel like him. Sometimes. In the way that every son feels like his father somewhere along the line, no matter how well he knows him. And I 'feel' like him in the other way too. I know that now. Which scares me a little.)

When Hynes sang the next line—'Look at me'—I opened my eyes and burst from the chair, finger to the ceiling. I made my way through the bar, singing, knocking into chairs, grabbing tables, paying no attention to the demands for me to shut the fuck up and sit down. My voice grew louder the closer I got to the stage, and Hynes didn't miss a beat. I'm sure it wasn't the first time a would-be accompanist staggered towards him onstage.

I don't know where the bouncer was. I don't know why any number of the guys I pissed off on my way through the place didn't stand and haul me back by the shoulders. But no one touched me. The syndrome, if I can call it that, of wanting to witness the wreckage rather than prevent it. Booker mustn't have seen me either. I wish he had.

I climbed onstage, took a stool and one of Hynes' guitars, sat down, and started strumming.

'Well it gets fairly uncertain up here, in this slippery spotlight my dear, been doing this for thirty odd years, still hardly quite there.'

He didn't stop me. He didn't acknowledge me either. The audience followed suit and remained quiet until the end of the song. In a way, it was a glorious moment. I was playing alongside Ron Hynes. I'd made it. Someone would post the performance on YouTube. It'd go viral. I'd get a million views, a million Likes. Fans would demand The River's Edge reunite. Wyatt and I would reconcile. Emerson would leave Bethy-Anne and divorce Jesus. Booker would postpone the philosophy. We'd be a band again. We'd sign a deal. Cut a record. Go on tour. Live the life.

But I knew even the moment I thought it that none of it was possible. I knew even as I sat on that stool on that stage that crashing Hynes' set ranked as one of the more *in*glorious moments of my life. Not that it helps, but I was so gassed I can barely remember the experience. Booker filled in some of the gaps, much to my shame, and someone actually did post a video on YouTube which filled in the rest. The video captures one of St. John's' finest hauling me to the ground, pinning me to the floor, and zip-tying my wrists behind my back. Memories of Eckleburg and her heavies. There haven't been a million views yet, but there have been enough, and the comments that follow aren't exactly resounding endorsements of my would-be music career.

Had I returned the guitar to its stand and stumbled offstage at the end of my duet, I might have avoided what was to come. But I've never really had a good sense of what it means to quit while I'm ahead. I always seem to take things a little too far.

Instead of taking a bow and my leave, I stood, guitar flung to my back, drove both hands in the air, and shouted, 'Rock on, St. John's.' Which is about when the video on YouTube begins.

I freed the mic from the stand and nearly swallowed it thanking my fans, telling them how great it was to be there.

'UmBenDunnoftheRiv'sEdge,' I said, 'andthisisMr.Ronfuck-inHyyynnnes.'

A chorus of boos.

'Heyheyhey, lilrespect, eh?'

Someone from the crowd: 'Who in the name of Jesus d'you think you are?'

'DinyouhearwhatIsaid?'

'We heard ya, ya stunned prick. Now get off the fuck'n stage.'

Someone grabbed the mic chord and yanked on it. I stumbled forward violently, but managed to right myself and yank back. The tug-of-war ended when the chord snapped in two, sending me into a backwards tumble. I tripped over an amp and went airborne. Time slowed. Or so it appears in the video. The cellphone videographer did a little editing before he uploaded the video, using some sort of slow-motion filter on the flight segment, fully capturing the awkwardness of my fall. The fear on my face turned to jarring pain the moment I landed. The guitar strapped to my back wasn't much of a cushion. Many of the viewers' comments rate this as one of the best parts of the video, second only to the policeman hauling me to the ground. Watching the reel, as I've done many times, I can see that I tried to brace myself, but there wasn't much I could do. I haven't the skill to manoeuvre myself in the air while I'm sober, let alone pissed drunk.

I lay there, moaning. Until this point Hynes had remained on his stool, calm and watching, forearms resting on the body of his guitar, not wanting, I can only assume, to get in the way of the debaucle, content to let this moment of Darwinian nature take its course. But as I'm flying through the air you can see him stand and lunge towards me, a hand outstretched. I like to think he was concerned for my wellbeing, but then I did have one of his guitars strapped to my back.

I remember everything from here on out. I remember him helping me up. I remember him telling me I should take this opportunity to leave quietly, while all parts of me were still assembled in some kind of human order, and not return. In the video you can see his hand on my shoulder, me nodding. Then my head goes up, like an animal alerted to danger. The guy I'd had the tug-of-war with was taunting me. On the video, you can hear him above the buzz of the place.

'Hey, Johnny Cash. Ya drunk fuck, ya.'

I was wearing black and I was drunk onstage. I didn't know who he was mocking more, me or Johnny Cash. Either way, I didn't like it. I swept Hynes' hand from my shoulder and marched forward. Like a swordsman from ancient Rome, I pulled the guitar from my back and struck the front of the stage with it, smashing the wooden body into splinters.

I've since replaced the guitar. I sent a note along with it, apologizing for my shameful Pete Townsend impersonation. To my great surprise I received a letter in return. I keep it in the top drawer of my desk and read it whenever I'm in need of a little brightening (which is more often than is likely normal). The letter reads: 'Dear Ben Dunn of the Riv's Edge: The guitar fits nicely in the stand you emptied. Thank you. As for your skills as a Townsend impersonator, they're second only to your skills as an orator. Also, for you, I suggest the activity of running over boxing. I do wish you the best of what's to come—Mr. Ron Fuck'n Hynes.'

Seemingly sober all of a sudden, I jumped down to floor level and struck the jeerer straight in the jaw. He fell backwards into the bracing arms of his friends and they threw him right back at me. I took two in the face and one in the stomach before I felt the policeman's hands on my shoulders. I was down again, forehead driven into the floor by a knee, hands wrenched behind my back, wrists zip-tied.

He hauled me up and escorted me through the place to a chorus of raucous applause and cheering—not exactly the kind of standing ovation I was going for.

Booker was still sitting at our table in the back. He didn't get up. The girls were huddled next to him, one on either side. He was smiling, an arm around each, like Hefner. I was able to stall my passage for a moment and catch his eye. He lifted his chin at me, gave a little shrug, put a hand to the side of his mouth, and called out, 'Nothing to be done.'

He was right, of course. There was nothing to be done.

I dropped my head and let the policeman steer me the rest of the way out into the cold dark night, back doors of the paddy wagon open wide, waiting to swallow me like a whale.

The bar had spilled into the street, cheering. The video was still running. I took a step up, my hands still tied behind my back, and the policeman shoved me in. I fell forward, landing on my right shoulder to protect my face. The pain was instant but dulled by the beer. It would wake me in the night, I knew. I managed to sit up and manoeuvre myself to the bench as the doors slammed shut. It was black and damp and smelled of metal and rain. I began to shiver and couldn't stop.

Through the small slit of a window as we pulled away I could see people jumping, a fog about them, fists driven towards the moon, faces distorted in furious bliss for the justice they believed they'd been part of and witness to. Like they'd just helped round up Bill Sikes or Raskolnikov. I can still hear them cheering.

Now, whenever I'm somewhere people shout appreciation, it's them I hear. My arbiters from The Rock. Damning. Bloodthirsty. Unforgiving.

At the police station I was relieved of my belt, my wallet, and my shoelaces. I stood at the counter and the senior officer behind the glass asked me questions. I was sober and aware of everything around me. Sober in the way those who are drunk far too often can make themselves believably lucid and articulate even when inebriated.

'State your full name and address.'

'Ben Fredrick Dunn.'

He waited.

'Address.'

'Well, sir, and I mean no disrespect, but that's not as easy to answer as it might seem.'

'And why is that, my son?'

The word 'son' stopped me. Through the glass I watched him open my wallet and take out my license.

'Forty-two Water St., Apartment B, Heron River, Ontario.'

'No.'

'What do you mean, no?'

'I don't live there anymore.'

'So where do you live then. A wad of dough like this doesn't put a man on the street.'

He fanned the fold of money I had in my wallet.

'It's not mine.'

His brow went up. 'So we can tack on theft to the rest of it.'

'It's my father's money. He gave it to me before he died. But I don't deserve it. I was a terrible son.'

'Do I look like a priest?'

'Wouldn't matter. I'm not Catholic. Thank Christ.'

He pointed a finger at me. 'Watch your language, you.'

'I've never really understood that expression.'

I felt a shove from behind. The one who'd zip-tied me. 'Don't get smart, you.'

I spoke over my shoulder. 'Envious?'

He hit me. I grabbed the back of my head, squinted. 'If my hands weren't tied—'

'What, tough guy. You'd what.'

The senior officer rapped the glass and furrowed his brow. 'That's enough.'

He folded his hands together and looked at me. I noticed the silver band so wedged into the flesh of his ring finger he'd have to cut it off should he ever want it removed. I imagined him at home with his family, at supper, in the living room watching the game, out back in the winter evenings playing shinny with his teenage sons on a rink he'd perfected over the years, his wife under the porch light, arms folded, calling them in for tea.

'Now, listen. I don't have all night to deal with you, so you'd better start cooperating or you'll find yourself in a far deeper pile than you already is.'

'Yes, sir.'

'So let's try again. What's your address?'

I sighed. 'Dun Laoghaire.'

I waited for him to ask me how to spell it. He didn't.

'I have an apartment there. Forty-two Harbour Court, Unit two, George's Place.'

He tapped away on his computer. Said nothing about the coincidence.

'Occupation.'

'Ex high school teacher.'

'*Current* occupation.'

'Don't you want to know why I said *ex*?'

'No, I do not. Now state your current occupation before I charge you with striking a police officer.'

'But I didn't strike—'

'You did if I says you did.'

'Sir. Yes, sir. I am currently unoccupied. Sir.'

He tapped something into the computer and spoke without looking at me. 'You really do fancy yourself a clever one, don't you?'

'Sir, no, sir.'

He smacked the last few keystrokes, smooshed his lips together, and backhanded the empty air.

'Yeah, well, whatever. I'll make the rest up later.'

Turning away, he drank from his mug and returned to his paper.

'Toss him in the tank.'

The one who'd zip-tied me grinned and grabbed the back of my neck. 'This way, you.'

I resisted. I didn't move. 'Tank? What tank?'

It hadn't occurred to me I'd actually have to spend the night in jail. I don't know what I thought when they took my wallet, my belt, and my shoelaces.

I tapped the glass. 'Excuse me, sir—sir?—sir?'

He kept his head down, flipped a page of his paper, slurped from his mug.

I wanted to reason with him. My pleas were polite and rational enough to start, but then the less-than-unruffled Ben Dunn took to the stage for a command performance undeserving of any kind of sympathy or understanding.

What Should a Man Do

Part II: Nothing to Do with Love

(a play: based on actual events and dialogue)

Lived out and written by Ben Dunn

Our pro-antagonist taps the glass. The senior officer does not look up.

BFD: Please, sir. If you'll give me a second to explain.

No response.

FB[27]: A second? My Jesus, he gave you a first, a second, a third, a fourth—

FB counts off his fingers.

BFD: Shut up. I wasn't talking to you.

FB: Shut up, eh. We'll see.

FB grabs BFD by the neck, turns him, and shoves him hard. BFD stumbles a step or two forward and does his best, which isn't much, to stay calm. He looks over his shoulder and calls out to the senior officer behind the glass.

BFD: Please, sir. This is all a huge misunderstanding.

FB shoves BFD again.

FB: Right out of her, you is. 'Magine. Crashing Ron Hynes. Sin. Some state. A night in the tank's the least you need.

BFD tries one more time, over his shoulder, to commission some sympathy, some leniency. As loud as he can manage.

---

[27] Fuzzy Bear. Booker's nickname for the officer who zip-tied me.

BFD: Sir. Please. I'm begging you. I'll do anything.

FB: My Jesus. Some pathetic you are.

FB shoves BFD again and BFD stumbles forward. Conceding, recognizing now that he's mired in a losing battle, he tips his head back, shuts his eyes, and calls out to the ceiling. Were his hands not secured behind his back he would have driven them, palms upward, over his head.

BFD: What did I do to deserve this?

FB laughs.

FB: Calling on the Lord now, he is. Listen to him.

Yelling, indignant.

BFD: Fuck the Lord. Fuck him to hell. And fuck you, too, you piss-ant.

FB crosses his chest, looks up.

FB: Forgive him, Father. He's out of his head.

BFD turns on FB and screams in his face.

BFD: I'm not out of my head. I'm right fuck'n in it.

Lips drawn tight, FB spins BFD around and drives both hands into his back, shoving him forward. They are in the corridor of holding cells. There are six. None are occupied. FB continues to direct BFD, forcefully, to the end of the corridor where he opens the last cell and shoves BFD in. FB grins as he clangs the cell door shut. He turns the key and walks away. BFD grabs the bars, yells.

BFD: Well, you caught me. Criminal mastermind of the century. Crackerjack fuck'n police work, gentlemen. I don't know how you did it. Call the papers. The streets are safer tonight.

No response. The place is quiet but for the mumble of officers talking in the distance, their muted laughter.

BFD: (*Shouting.*) You think this is funny?

No response.

BFD: Hey! I'm talking to you! Answer me!

Nothing again but distant, indiscernible banter.

BFD: You want to know something? You're the fucking joke. This whole place is a fucking joke.

Then to himself, shaking his head, serious and revelatory.

BFD: This is a joke. It has to be. There's been some kind of mistake. There's no way I'm supposed to be here.

Louder, hands clutching the bars, face pressed against them, on the verge of tears.

BFD: Hey! Listen to me! I'm not supposed to be here!

Behind him comes a voice. Calm, without judgement.

A Voice: Where are you supposed to be?

BFD spins around.

BFD: Who was that? Who's there?

A Voice: You don't recognize my voice?

BFD backs against the wall. Sitting on the bench is the ghost of his father. (There is no other word for what he sees.)

BFD: It can't be.

Ghost: Maybe not. But it is.

BFD: But you're—

GHOST: Dead. I know.

BFD laughs. Nervous. Incredulous.

BFD: Sorry.

GHOST: Don't be.

BFD: It's just—

GHOST: Unexpected. I can imagine.

BFD laughs again. Drives his palms into his eyes and shakes his head.

BFD: I've gone mad.

GHOST: Don't flatter yourself, son. You're not mad. You're intoxicated. And you're full of guilt. Which is never a good combination.

BFD: You're a manifestation. You're not really here.

GHOST: To you I am.

BFD: To me.

GHOST: Yes. Which is all that really matters.

BFD: You know, you don't sound like him.

GHOST: I don't?

BFD: No.

GHOST: Whom do I sound like?

BFD shakes his head.

BFD: I don't know. But not him.

GHOST: Well, strictly speaking, I'm not him. I'm an ethereal representation of him.

BFD: See? There's no way my father says something like that.

GHOST: Right. Okay. I'll speak plainly then. I'm a ghost.

BFD looks at his socked feet and wiggles his toes. He smirks, folds his arms over his chest, and decides to play along.

BFD: Alright. Tell me then. So I know how to describe you to the therapist who's surely in my future. What type of ghost would you say you are, Dickensian or Shakespearian?

GHOST: Canadian.

BFD: Hah.

BFD looks over his shoulder for an audience that isn't there.

BFD: A funny ghost. You don't very often hear of a funny ghost.

GHOST: Allow me to explain.

BFD: Please. I can't wait.

GHOST: If a Dickensian ghost effects guilt and regret, and a Shakespearian ghost incites guilt and vengeance, then a Canadian ghost brings about guilt and apology. You're full of guilt, son, and you're weighed down by the need for apology.

BFD's face goes straight. He nods.

BFD: You know, it's amazing. You look exactly like him. Not the older version of him, not the version I remember. More like the twenty-year-old version I know from pictures.

The ghost smiles. BFD folds his arms.

BFD: Can I ask you something?

GHOST: Shoot.

BFD: Why did you love her? I mean, how could you love her even after she left?

GHOST: I'm not sure I can answer that. Love is for the living.

BFD: I don't think so. I'm living and I've never come close to understanding it.

GHOST: It's not something to be understood.

BFD: That's what's frustrating. It's a thing without reason. We're given brains to think with and hearts to feel with. But the brain is useless when it comes to love and technically all a heart does is pump blood. Which has nothing to do with love.

GHOST: Seems to me—and I may be speaking out of turn here—that blood has everything to do with love.

BFD turns towards the sound of someone being brought in: a loud, distorted version of a voice he thinks he recognizes. He can picture the detainee at the counter, hands zip-tied behind his back, the frustrated senior officer behind the glass casting him off with a raised brow and a disinterested flip of the fingers. Although he's been here less than an hour, BFD feels like an old hand at hard time.

When he looks at the bench again, the ghost is gone and BFD is left to wonder if he imagined it all. He sits on the floor, knees at his chest, and hugs his legs. He closes his eyes and thinks of the last time he visited his father.

BFD: I'm so sorry.

GHOST: (*somewhere beyond the cell*) I know, son. I know you are. But there's no need. There's no need.

BFD feels the water well within his eyes, feels his throat tighten. He breathes deeply and when he looks, FB is standing in front of his cell. For a moment he thinks the voice of the ghost may have been the officer, mocking him. He does his best to regain himself.

BFD: Is there something I can help you with?

FB: Not likely.

BFD: Right. I forgot. Simianity and asininity are incurable conditions.

FB squints and shakes his head a little.

FB: Huh?

BFD: Exactly.

FB crosses his arms.

FB: Least I'm not huddled up on the floor of a cell muttering to himself like some fuck'n nutter.

BFD pushes himself to his feet.

BFD: Unless you're here to let me out, fuck off and leave me alone.

FB: Ah, now that's not a very nice thing to say to the man who brought your misery a bit of company.

FB nods in the direction of the cell next to BFD's.

FB: Says he knows you. Poor bastard.

BFD grabs the bars, but not desperately, and speaks through them.

BFD: Who's there?

A VOICE: Knock, knock.

BFD: Booker?

BOOKER: No, no, no. We messed it up. I'm supposed to say 'Booker.' You're supposed to say, 'Booker Who?' Then I'm supposed say, 'Booker's what you didn't do which is why you're penned up in here.'

BFD grins.

BFD: Sorry. I seem to be missing all my Qs tonight.

BOOKER: You're forgiven. So long as you mind your Ps. I don't want to hear about you pissing yourself in the night.

FB's eyes flick back and forth between the two cells. BFD and BOOK-ER trade quips as though they're sitting across from one another at a table in a bar.

BFD: Ah, now, you shouldn't Ts.

BOOKER: But it comes with such Es.

BFD: Gs. You can be such an Rs.

BOOKER: I prefer Ys guy.

BFD thinks a moment, shrugs, concedes.

BFD: I'm out. You win.

Booker rattles the bars and lets out a whoop in mock celebration.

BFD: Listen, wise guy. What are you doing in here, anyway?

BOOKER: Envy. I couldn't stand the thought of you being able to tell the story of spending a night in jail with me left to imagine it.

Arms crossed, FB shakes his head.

FB: Nutters, the pair of you. Should've bypassed the joint and taken the two of you's straight to the looney bin.

BOOKER: Ah, see that, Ben Franklin? Fuzzy Bear's trying to play along. Must feel all alone out there in the free world. Look at him.

BOOKER directs his next line in earnest to FB.

BOOKER: I have to tell you, though, Mr. Bear, I wish you'd said, 'We should've taken the Ws straight to the loonie bin.' I'd've been really impressed then.

Confused, FB furrows his brow, flips Booker off, and leaves. Booker calls after him.

BOOKER: Clever. I'll have to remember that one.

A moment goes by.

BFD: Hey.

BOOKER: Hey yourself.

BFD: Thanks.

BOOKER: Don't thank me. Completely selfish on my part. Now when I introduce The Outsider to those yawning first-years I can begin with something genuine like, 'Now, don't get me wrong, I'm not condoning criminal activity, but ever since I spent a night in jail I've been able to relate to Camus' protagonist in a much more authentic manner.' Instant respect. I should be thanking you.

BFD: We should get a picture. Authenticate the moment.

BOOKER: Maybe we can convince Fuzzy Bear to pose for a shot, him with his gun drawn and pointed at you with your arms up, me behind him, a chair above my head, ready to come crashing down.

BFD: I'm not sure he'd go for it. He seems a little less than taken with us.

BOOKER: A little faith. I can be very convincing.

BFD nods. Another lost gesture.

BFD: You saw the fine display that put *me* in here. What'd you do?

BOOKER: A few minutes after they took you away, I came staggering out of the bar, beer in hand, singing 'Dirty Old Town,' naked as the day I was born.

BFD: Naked.

BOOKER: I shouldn't exaggerate. I was wearing boots and a toque. Oh, and a scarf. It is December in St. John's after all.
BFD: What'd you do with your clothes?

BOOKER: The girls took them.

BFD shakes his head.

BFD: Unbelievable.

BOOKER: When I told them what I planned to do, they said they wanted to help. I told them I'd been undressing myself for years and was sure, even though I'd had a few pints, I'd be able to manage on my own.

BFD laughs.

BOOKER: So then they say, 'Okay, give us your clothes. We'll hold onto them for you.' I say, 'Great. But how do I know you're not just going to take them and put them up on Kijiji item by item and use my campus celebrity to make a quick buck?'

BFD: What'd they say?

BOOKER: They crossed their hearts and promised not to.

BFD: Hah!

BOOKER: I know. I said, 'What good's a promise in this day and age? I need something concrete.' So the one called Monica went and got a Sharpie from the bar. 'Give me a cheek,' she says.

BFD: You're making this up.

BOOKER: Nope.

BFD: So what'd you do?

BOOKER: I undid my jeans and gave her a cheek.

BFD: Jesus. You didn't.

BOOKER: I did. And without hesitation she Sharpied her name and her roommate's name and their numbers right on the cheek of my ass, a little heart at the end for punctuation.

BFD: What's her roommate's name?

BOOKER: Rachel.

BFD shakes his head, smiles.

BFD: See, now I know you're lying.

BOOKER: What.

BFD: Monica and Rachel? Come on. Plus, unless you have some innate ability to sense the shape of individual letters being written on your skin, or unless you have some freakish ability to see your own ass—which I don't want to know about if you do— there's no way you could tell what she wrote.

BOOKER: Au contraire, mon frère. When she was finished she held up a little makeup mirror for me to check—I can show you when we get out if you'd like.

BFD holds a hand up like a stop sign and shakes his head—again, gestures his friend cannot see.

BFD: I'll take your word for it.

BOOKER: Suit yourself.

BFD: I should say the same to you.

BOOKER: Good one.

BFD: I have to ask. If you were, uh, you know, *denuded* when they picked you up, what are you now?

BOOKER: De-Davided. Apparently I'm no statue. They wrapped me in a trenchcoat. I look like a Goddamn flasher.

A moment goes by.

BFD: I always thought that son of a bitch Richards looked like a flasher. Maybe I can pin that on him.

BOOKER: Too difficult to get proof.

BFD: Christ, I wouldn't want any proof.

BOOKER: Listen, you really want to crush this guy?

BFD: Yes. I do. I really do.

BOOKER: Okay then. Answer me this. What do people want more than anything else in the world?

BFD: Money.

BOOKER: Besides money.

BFD: Fame.

BOOKER: Close. Recognition.

BFD nods.

BOOKER: So. What kind of recognition would a self-loving, acknowledgement-seeking pedagogue like Richards covet more than anything else?

BFD: I don't know.

BOOKER: Think big.

A moment goes by. BFD snaps his fingers and points to the empty hall beyond his cell.

BFD: There's a Governor General's Award for teachers. He'd fuck'n love that.

BOOKER: Perfect. There's your bait.

BFD: There's my bait.

BOOKER: Trick him somehow into thinking they're giving him the award, then whammo—

Booker stomps the cell floor with his boot.

BOOKER: —you crush him.

BFD drives a fist into an open palm.

BFD: I crush him.

A moment goes by.

BFD: And how do I do that?

BOOKER: Good question. And right now, I have to be honest, I don't know the answer. (*Yawns.*) What I do know is I'm drunk and fuck'n exhausted and these cots don't look half bad.

BFD yawns, too.

BFD: We'll sleep on it then.

They both lie down on their respective cots within their respective cells.

BOOKER: Tomorrow we scheme.

BFD grins.

BFD: Perchance we'll dream.

BOOKER: Ah, yes. For who knows in this sleep, my chum, what schemes may come.

The awkwardness of afterwards was unavoidable, but there was something in between the *during* and the *after* that bordered on perfection. My hands were on her waist, hers my shoulders. Foreheads touching, our breathing slowed and our hearts thumped a little more softly.

When we finally came apart, we were like soldiers in the moments after an explosion: heads down, disoriented, scouring the ground for our belongings, parts of ourselves, so focussed on practical details like the whereabouts of our thrown clothes that everything beyond our immediate vision was a blurr, unimportant.

Neither of us said a thing.

When I finally looked at her again, she was standing at the door fully dressed for the cold. She seemed put together in a way I'd never been.

She stood there, a hand on the door, a bag over her shoulder, waiting. I pulled on my toque and hoodie and headed towards her. She opened the door and turned off the lights. I followed her out.

She looked up at the spectral moon. 'You're going to freeze.'

I hunched my shoulders, crossed my arms. 'I'll be alright.'

The streetlights were on and it was beginning to snow. People walked by in both directions. Lives continued.

She looked past me, down the street. Checked her watch. Adjusted the bag on her shoulder. Her breath punctuated the air.

It was quiet between us and then we both spoke—

Me: 'Listen, I was wondering . . .'

Her: 'Well, I should be going . . .'

—the 'ings' blending together so that neither of us really heard what the other had said.

Me again, hopeful: 'Sorry?'

She looked at her watch. 'No, it's just—I should probably be going.'

'Right. Getting late, I guess.'

She looked at her boots, then into the street. A bus passed by. She smiled, sort of, and turned to leave.

'Wait—'

I stepped towards her, touched her arm. She could barely feel it through her coat, I'm sure, but it was enough to make her stop and look at my hand.

She looked right at me. God, how I wish there was some way to go back there right now so I could say what I wanted to say, so I could say something at least, convince her not to go, to come with me to St. John's, to consider the chance of us.

'Aislinn, I—'[28]

She continued to look at me and waited. I exhaled, pocketed my hands. She grinned with one side of her mouth, tilted her head before shaking it.

'Oh, Ben.' She touched my face with her gloved hand. 'You see? You're not real.'

I furrowed my brow. 'Not real?'

She spoke calmly. If anything, there was a hint of sadness in her voice, sympathy even. 'You're a phantom. You don't really exist.'

I displayed each of my hands, looked at the palms, the backs, touched my head, my chest, my legs. 'Funny. Feels like I exist.'

'That's not what I mean, Ben.'

'Seems to me I was real enough ten minutes ago, or are you in the habit of fucking ghosts?'

She didn't get upset. She had every right to, but she didn't.

'You're angry.'

'Yeah, a little.'

'It's complicated.'

'What's complicated?'

'This.'

'What, you and I?'

'There is no you and I, Ben. That's what's complicated.'

---

[28] '—I love you.' Why didn't I just say it?

I pretended not to hear what she said.

'You know, I don't mind that you have a kid.'

She sort of laughed. 'That makes it so much easier. Having your approval.'

'That's not what I meant.'[29]

She crossed her arms, sighed. 'We were only together for a few days. Seven years ago. A blip in time. It's become a dream I sometimes let myself replay. But that's all it is, Ben. A dream.'

'What about right now?'

'What about it?'

'You're going to tell me there's nothing here?'

'It's not that simple.'

'Yes. It is.'

The wind picked up a little and tossed the snow around like in a glass globe. She was beautiful in it. Beautiful.

I looked into the street, then at her. 'Can I ask you something?'

She shrugged, but not dismissively.

'Are you happy?'

'I am.'

'And you think I would make you unhappy.'

'No. I just don't want anything to change.'

'Things change every day. Sameness is an illusion.'

She shrugged again. 'That may be so, but I'm content within the illusion.'

I stepped towards her. I wanted to touch her. I wanted to hold onto her.

'I don't want to lose you again.'

'You never had me, Ben.'

'That's not what I meant.'

'It was just sex.'

But it wasn't, and even as she said it, I knew she didn't believe it.

I let my hands drop, sighed my concession. She stepped in and kissed me.

---

[29] I meant I knew he was mine and I was okay with it. I was more than okay.

'Goodbye, Ben.'

She turned, without pause, and walked away.[30]

---

[30] Just like that. You turned and walked away. How could I not run after you? I wish now that I hadn't. I wish I'd let you go. I wish I'd given myself time to think. I didn't mean to grab you the way I did. I didn't mean to scare you. God, the look on your face. How can I undo that moment? How can I erase it? Please. Tell me. How?

In the morning my head was heavier than usual and my mouth was so dry I couldn't speak, which I discovered when I tried to say Booker's name. I guzzled the little box of room-temperature juice sitting next to the mayonnaise-smeared plastic-wrapped sandwich on the floor just inside the cell. Prison fare. The thought of taking a bite of the sandwich made me nauseous. I stood, a little shaky, approached the the bars, and said Booker's name a few more times. He didn't respond. By eight-thirty, FB had opened our cell doors and said we were free to go.

'Hey, Snow White. Wake up.'

I watched FB try to rouse my friend who somehow continued to sleep.

'Listen. Whatever I said last night, whatever I did—'

'I wouldn't worry about it none.' He didn't look at me. 'I doled out my share. Goes with the territory.'

I nodded and that was it.

Booker finally began to stir. He stretched and made waking noises, put a lot of effort into it. Then he sat on the edge of the cot, rubbed his eyes, and let out a monster of a yawn.

'I was just having the most amazing dream.'

He was wearing a trenchcoat and boots, like he'd said. His shins were showing.

'I was a World War Two spy who looked like Robert Redford in his Sundance days. I'd just had sex with Eva Braun who bore a striking resemblance to Diane Keaton from the first Godfather, all innocent but not. Afterwards we sat up in bed and I poured us each a Macallan's. We smoked and drank like we had no other place to be. At one point Eva-Diane unfolded a real artsy looking map of Berlin. *Here*, she said. *It's here*. Meaning old Adolf's secret lair. I clinked her glass with mine and said, in a real cool but natural Sean Connery voice, *Always do what you are afraid to do*. Then I slipped two bullets into the housing of a long-barrelled silver pistol and fired once at the ceiling. Eva-Diane leaned in and inhaled the smoke through her nose like it was the best thing she'd ever smelled. She looked up at me and I kissed her, all big and dramatic, the way they did in old black and white films. It was brilliant. Then she started yelling at me in English, *Hey, Snow White. Wake up*. I assume that was one of you two.'

Grinning, I folded my arms.

'Anyway, it was pretty realistic. You think something like that could've really happened?'

FB shook his head. Emphatically. 'Not a chance. There's no way Hitler would've told the missus where his hideout was and if he ever took her there, he'd've blindfolded her for sure.'

I grinned. 'Like a visitor to the bat cave.'

FB looked at me.

'Ignore him,' Booker said. 'Please. Continue.' He could be so serious when he wanted to be.

Still looking at me, FB said, 'He was no fuck'n Batman, let me tell you.' Then to Booker: 'Plus, he'd never've let Braun roam free like that.'

'You don't think so?'

'I know it. I've read two books on the man.'

'Two. Well.' Booker folded his arms, feigned deference. FB checked over his shoulder, continued to speak to Booker.

'Want to know the truth?'

'I do. Yes.'

FB leaned in and put the back of his hand like a shield to the side of his mouth: a ten-year-old imparting the secret password to a new member of the club. 'He never took those cyanide tablets.'

'Really.'

'Nope. Two SS snuck him out in the middle of the night and ferried him off into the hills.'

'You don't say.'

'Well, they never found his body, did they?'

'I don't know.'

'Trust me. They didn't.'

'If you say so.'

'I do.'

The whole time they were talking, Booker was moving FB in a slow circle. By the end, FB's back was to the rear of the cell. Booker took one quick step backwards and clanged the door shut. It locked automatically.

'Hey! What the hell are you doing?'

Standing there in his trenchcoat and boots, Booker put one hand on his hip and the back of the other to his forehead. 'All is not well. I doubt some foul play.'

FB grabbed the bars. 'You'd better let me out of here right now.'

Booker shook his head, brushed one index finger with the other. 'Tsk. Tsk. Such attitude.'

FB pointed a finger at him through the bars. He spoke quietly, sternly. 'Listen, you son of a bitch. If you don't let me out of here—'

Booker stepped up to the cell, smirking. 'You'll what? Scream? Rattle your cage? That wouldn't look very good. Having the tables turned on you by a couple of drunks. Or what'd you call us? Fuck'n nutters, I think it was. Besides, shouldn't you have a key?'

FB patted his pants, then his shirt. He turned in the cell, looked on the ground, under the pillow, under the cot, behind the toilet. When he looked at us again, Booker was dangling the big, movie-style keyring right in front of the bars.

'This what you're looking for?'

FB grinned and nodded. 'Okay. Very funny. You got me. Now can I please have those keys?'

Booker continued to hold the keyring in the air. He looked down, drummed the fingers of his free hand on his closed mouth. He shook his head and looked at FB. 'Sorry. Lost in thought. What is it you said?'

'I said, can I have those keys, please?'

'No. I don't think so.'

Booker set the keyring on the floor, out of reach. 'I'll leave them here. You'll figure something out. You could use your belt like a catch. Or maybe your pants. They'd be heavier. But then again you wouldn't want to be caught in here with your pants down. What would the Chief think?' Booker looked at me. 'Is that the right title? Chief?'

I shrugged.

He looked at FB. 'No matter.'

Then he turned and left.

I followed him. I could hear FB behind me, whisper-screaming for me to help. I ignored him, which I feel a little bad about now, considering we had sort of made amends.

.   .   .

Booker crossed his naked shins, leaned an elbow on the front desk, and clasped his hands. 'Booker and Dunn. Cells five and six. Checking out.'

The woman at the desk didn't look at us and she didn't smile. Booker patted the pockets of his trenchcoat.

'I seem to have misplaced my room key. I don't know if Benjamin here has his.'

He looked at me. I shook my head, grinned.

'Nope. He doesn't have his either. I hope that's not a problem.'

She clacked away on the computer, spun her chair away, and went into another room. When she returned, she had two large transparent bags, sealed. She handed us the bags and directed us to sign our names beside the Xs she indicated with her pen. All without looking at or speaking to us.

'The bed was comfortable enough, but the rooms were a little draughty and the food somewhat bland. And I do have to say, the service personnel—present company excluded of course—was lacking in all class, intellect, and amiability. I'm not sure I'd recommend the place, but we sure do appreciate St. John's' finest putting us up for the night.'

Booker examined the pen he'd used to sign his name.

'Mind if I keep this? It is an exquisite pen. So fluid. See, my colleague and I are writing a little screenplay. The ideas really started to flow last night, but neither of us had anything to write with. We weren't allowed writing utensils in our rooms. The concierge took them when we checked in. I'm not blaming him, mind you. I do understand. There was a distinct possibility we'd've stabbed ourselves with them in the middle of the night. Or, more likely still, we may have added to the graffiti on the walls, the presence of which suggests one of two things: one, that the no-pen rule is new, or two, previous boarders were able to sneak pens in by squeezing them between their buttocks. I should've thought of that. At any rate, I have to say, some of the writing our predecessors managed to leave for us was quite thought-provoking and served as excellent bedtime reading.'

He put the pen down on the counter and made a square with his thumbs and index fingers. He drew his head back, closed an eye, and pretended to line up a shot with the woman at the desk as the focal point.

'Yes. I definitely see a part in our film for you. The sexy policewoman. An Elmore Leonard type character. Like Karen Sisco. Hardnosed when she has to be, with a soft-spot for gentleman cons. '

She reached out and took the pen. Booker put one hand on his hip, touched his chin.

'No to the pen. Okay. I understand. But listen, do you have a card or something? You know, so we can get in touch when the script is finished and casting begins.'

As she spun her chair away I thought I might have seen her smile a little, but I couldn't be sure. I took Booker by the arm and walked him towards the main entrance. He didn't resist. Before stepping into the revolving door, he called one last time over his shoulder.

'Okay then, Karen. We'll see you on set.'

When we walked outside, I ripped into my Personals bag, pulled on my toque and hoodie, laced my shoes (undone as I was) and pocketed my wallet. Booker had nothing in his bag but the shoelaces from his boots, his ID, and a scarf. He tore it open, shoved the laces and the ID in his trenchcoat pocket, and wrapped the scarf stylishly about his neck.

'I know a place,' he said, and began to walk with unwavering purpose, 'that serves Irish coffee before noon.'

.   .   .

I convinced him to stop at a surplus store along the way. I
bought him a pair of pants, a sweater, and a toque. I bought
myself a coat. There was a deal on gloves. I bought two pair.
Outside, we slid the gloves on and batted them together in
unintentional unison.

'There,' I said. 'Like new men.'

'More like surplus men.'

I laughed. 'Yes. Unnecessary, excessive, redundant.'

'You're forgetting *spare*.'

'Yes. Spare. Spare is better.'

We walked, snow crunching under our boots, and breathed
in the cold crisp air. Booker put on his best Eliot and I smiled to
myself as he recited the spur-of-the-moment revision.

'We are the spare men. We are the abundant men. Walking
together, headpiece filled with barley. Alas! Our dried throats,
when we cough together, are like desert ash. Or elephant skin or
burnt-out grass in July's dry field. This is the way the day begins.
This is the way the day begins. This is the way the day begins.
Not with a bang, but a glimmer.'

.   .   .

The place Booker took me was full of people who looked
the way I felt and all of a sudden I didn't feel so bad. Some of the
guilt was gone. Some of the headache was gone. Some of the
regret and the yearning to undo the things I knew I could not
undo were gone. I felt better. Where a man is, is everything.

Booker put two fingers in the air as he sat. Soon there were
two steaming mugs in front of us, followed shortly by two plates
of food.

'I've always loved the name Bangers and Mash. It sounds so
wrong, but tastes so good.'

I nodded, closed my eyes with another mouthful of the hot
Irish coffee. Warmth all the way down. We ate in near silence, the
food settling in our stomachs the way a welcome snowfall covers

the muck and grime of a recent and unwanted thaw. Everything was good again.

'So. In the case where one man might wish to crush another man—'

I grinned, wiped my mouth, and leaned forward on the table.

'—here's what the crushing man should do.'

Now Might I Do It

Before we get to the business of my revenge, I want to go back to the night of the band's reunion gig in Heron River, which was just about a year ago as I sit here and write this. Having read what I've written so far, I feel there are three things in particular which I need to clear up: the Chantal incident, for one; two, how Richards came by his so-called video evidence of my alleged marijuana trafficking (to students no less, which had to be what led Eckleburg to seek out the other six testimonies she claimed to have); and three, how I managed, with said evidence against me, to elude being formally charged and convicted.

First off, I still contend I was not in the wrong, morally or otherwise, for sleeping with Chantal Aster that night. It was consensual and it was just the once. What's more, I was soon privy to some information that stopped me cold from pursuing her any further. A little more than a week after our encounter, I was standing at the door of my fall semester grade twelve English class, welcoming a fresh crop of fleetingly eager, device-thumbing students, and in she walks, Chantal, books in hand. I was stunned, to say the least, though she was strangely calm. Maybe she'd known I was a teacher (*I know who you are, Mr. Dunn*) and was therefore able to prepare herself well in advance. Who knows? But *I* certainly wasn't prepared. I could feel the blood rush to my face, the sweat rise on my skin. Other than the initial flicker of recognition in her eyes, she didn't let on she knew me at all. I got hold of myself and did my best to follow her lead. Sitting down in my class that day she still seemed at least twenty-five.

Anyway, it may seem curious that I didn't recognize her that night at the bar if she was a student from my school. A fair concern. Heron River is a small town, and although small town teachers don't know every student in the school, by the time grade twelve rolls around most teachers are able to recognize, at the very least, most of the graduating class. There's a simple explanation for why I didn't recognize Chantal Aster. She was a transfer student from a school in the city. Her parents, married since law school, were market savvy and had managed to accumulate a small fortune by the time they'd both reached the ripe old age of forty-four. They were both intelligent, left-thinking, free-spirited book lovers who believed in independence at an early age, and they had raised a beautiful daughter who I'd describe in the very same way. Jonathon and Karen Aster had always promised each other that when they could afford it, they'd quit the practice of law, move to a small town north of the city, and open a bookshop. Early retirement, easy living, and exposure for their daughter to a different sort of world. Not quite rural, not quite suburban. Something of its own yet to be named. So, in the summer of 2009, they bought the spot on the main drag of Heron River that used to be a second-hand clothing store called Second Best. It had just gone out of business. According to the locals and other store-owners, the Asters' timing was perfect. Second Best was the one blight on an otherwise trendy, touristy, middle-to-upper-scale string of main street shops that drew weekend and holiday traffic from at least an hour away in every direction. And during the nicer weather business was booming almost every day. After a month of renovations Jonathon and Karen Aster opened Pages for business. It was an uncluttered, modern, welcoming place. On my first visit I bought an anthology of Shakespeare's soliloquies (clichéd, I know) and introduced myself. I liked the Asters right away and they seemed to like me. I think I may have even invited them to the reunion gig. God, if only they'd come. Imagine. I returned to the store a number of times over the summer and we talked at length about books and education and how they'd ended up in Heron River. Some of the less conversational details (their mid-forties windfall, for example) came, and continue to come, from my old friend the restaurateur, Emerson McKnight. He keeps me apprised of the goings-on in Heron River. Has his thumb on the pulse of every little tidbit, gossip or otherwise, that's flung around town. Always has. He's a master of being in the know.[31]

Back to the night in question. First off, I had no reason to believe Chantal Aster was underage. She looked and acted twenty-five. Second, she was the one who came on to me. It didn't take long for me to bite, mind you, but she was the one to initiate things. From there the night proceeded as those kinds of nights do. Tension built between us, and from the outset we both knew how the night would end. During the band's last set I called her up onstage and she sang a song with the band like we'd arranged. The crowd loved it. We couldn't have had a better final show (minus the Wyatt incident). Last call came around, the bar started to clear out, and by the time the lights were up she was still there.

The place was empty save for Chantal, me, Booker, and the bar owner, Hank. Wyatt, of course, had taken off before our last set, and because Emerson had to get home to Miss Elizabeth-Anne he had left with the last of our audience. I knew Hank pretty well, so it was easy getting more drinks. I followed Chantal to a booth in the back. We sat beside each other, I made some stupid toast, and we drank. It wasn't long before we started up. Pretty heavily too. Booker and Hank were at the bar. I could hear them, but their banter was distant. I don't know how long we were in that booth but it was three in morning before we all finally left.

Chantal said she had to use the ladies' room. Hank let her back in and waited for her inside. Booker and I waited out front where we lit one up. After a couple of pulls each, I heard someone call my name.

'Dunn! Hey Dunn!'

---

[31] Why bother to include all this here. Especially considering Chantal's parents are both book lovers, not to mention book sellers, and will likely have their eyes on these pages one day if they're ever bound together as a book themselves. But as I mentioned earlier, more than anything this is an admission I'm writing and the Chantal business is something I feel I need to admit to. Besides, her parents don't put me in mind of the type of people who'd get upset or pursue any sort of retribution once they knew all the details. And they're bound to find out sooner or later. This is as good a way as any.

There were always a few stragglers this time of night. I squinted but couldn't tell who it was until the caller and his two friends were standing with us under the bar's exterior lights.

It was Dean. I didn't recognize the other two.

'Would you look at this. The upstanding Mr. Dunn, standing outside a bar at three in the morning. Tugging on a J no less.'

I grinned and shook his hand. What else could I do?

'If it isn't Master Dean King. And how does this midsummer's night find you?'

'Well, Mr. Dunn, it finds me well. But I do believe it's summer's end, not mid, and it's been a while since I had a dream.'

I grinned again and introduced him to Booker, who stashed the joint we were working on between his lips and shook the boy's hand, squinting through the smoke, half-smirking. Dean immediately reminded Booker of himself at that age, I could tell, though he'd never say so.

Dean's friends were from the city, which seemed to fit, and he told us that after having spent the last few hours at the Emerald Room they were in the mood for a little stroll through town.

'We were, in fact, headed to Rafter Park to enjoy a length or two of our own rolled tea when I caught sight of you, Mr. Dunn.'

Dean felt the pockets of his cargo shorts, front and back, tapped his t-shirted chest with both hands.

'Ah, would you look at that. I've gone and left the goods at home.'

He stuffed his hands in his pockets and smiled. He wavered a little, standing there, but it was difficult for me to discern his level of drunkenness because of my own state of inebriation, not to mention how impressively articulate he was.

'Well, you boys'll just have to breathe deep and inhale the intoxicating aroma of the park's summer flowers.'

'Ah, come on now, Dunn. I can appreciate a lily or a rose as much as the next guy, but my friends here are in a religious mood and I promised them some Mother Mary.'

Booker laughed.

'What do you say, Mr. Dunn?'

I shook my head. 'Sorry, I can't.'

'No need to apologize. But I have to ask, why not?'

'You know why.'

'I have to say—I don't.'

For some reason I lowered my voice. 'Listen, Dean. I can't do it.'

'Sure you can, Mr. Dunn. I believe in you.'

'Jesus, Dean. I can't. You're a student.'

Booker clapped me on the back. 'We're all students, Ben Franklin.'

A spark of kinship flashed in Dean's eyes as he looked past me to Booker.

'I like the way your friend thinks, Mr. Dunn. He's very— perspicacious.'

Booker pointed at Dean. 'Hah! I like this fucking kid.'

Encouraged, Dean continued. 'See? We're all friends here, Mr. Dunn. Besides, I'm not technically your student for another week and a half. I'm just a fellow strider in the night looking for a friendly gesture.'

I sighed.

Grinning, joint between his lips, Booker motioned for me to share some of our stash with Dean. What could I do?

'Listen, you never got these from me, and if anyone ever comes asking, I'll deny it outright.'

I looked over my shoulder and down the street, slid two joints from my pocket, and slipped them to Dean.

'Ah, that's grand, Mr. Dunn. Grand.' He tucked one behind his ear and gave the other to his friends. 'You're a gentleman and a scholar.'

I pointed at him. 'This never happened.'

He shrugged. 'What never happened?'

'I must be fucking crazy.'

'Oh, I almost forgot.' He reached into his back pocket, took me by the wrist, slapped two bills into my hand, and held them there. 'For your troubles and your kindness, sir.'

Without looking at the money, I stuffed it in my back pocket, did a quick check over both shoulders, and looked up and down the street.

'Jesus Christ, what are you doing?'

'What.'

'Handing me money like that.'

Dean laughed. I shook my head, furrowed my brow.

'Ah, come on, Dunn.'

I looked across the street at Joe's Pizza. The neon sign was still on. Someone was standing on the balcony above the restaurant with his hands out over the railing like he was about to catch a ball. When he saw me looking at him, he pulled his hands in, turned, and vanished into the apartment. The figure on the balcony struck me as a little odd, but I didn't really think much of it at the time. Little did I know.

Dean put both hands on my shoulders and looked me straight in the eyes. There was no doubt he was drunk. We all were.

'It's cool, Dunn. It was just a joke.'

I pulled the bills out and held them under the light.

'See? Canadian Tire money.'

I nodded.

'You were sure quick to pocket it though.'

'Yeah, well, I didn't want anybody seeing.'

I handed it back.

'Nah, you keep it.'

I folded the bills and slid them back in my pocket. 'I'll put it towards a coffee mug.'

'So, we're okay then?'

I nodded again.

He pointed at me. 'You're a good man, Dunn.[32] I owe you one.'

I looked at him. I was serious. 'You don't owe me a God damn thing. Understand?'

He nodded.

Sounding strangely paternal all of sudden, I told him to go enjoy the rest of his summer and I'd see him in September. He

---

[32] Not something I've heard very often. But I want you to know—despite and in light of all the evidence here—I'm trying to be. I am trying.

extended a hand and I shook it, nodded to his friends. He shook Booker's hand, too, who grinned approvingly.

He spoke as he started away. 'If we shadows have offended, think but this and all is mended, that you have slumbered here, while we visions did appear, and so to you we apparitions seem no more than the end of summer's dream.'

He turned and was gone. Into the night.

Booker passed me the joint we'd been sharing, and I took a final pull before rubbing it out under my shoe.

'Smart little fucker, isn't he?'

I nodded. 'Like someone else I know.'

'Ah, well,' he said, looking into the sky, 'he'll find it doesn't pay. People come to expect too much.'

I looked at Booker and it was the first time I'd ever felt something like sympathy for him. Then I heard Chantal and in an instant I shifted focus.

'God, I'm sorry I took so long. I just wanted to freshen up a little and then I couldn't find my ID or my money and I was *freaking* but Hank here calmed me down and was kind enough to help me look around the place—we looked everywhere, didn't we—and would you believe the whole time the money was tucked right in here' —she slipped the money out of her bra to show us, then slipped it back in— 'and my ID was in my back pocket. Too much to drink, I guess. Ruins your short-term memory.'

Chantal took me by the hand, went on her toes, and kissed me. Booker stuck a hand in the air as he and Hank walked away.

'Till it be morrow, my Montague chum.'

I grinned. Chantal and I held hands as we walked across the street.

'Why did he call you Montague?'

I shook my head. 'That's just Booker being Booker.'

'Funny, it sounded like Booker being Shakespeare.'

I nodded. 'You like Shakespeare?'

She bit her bottom lip. 'I love Shakespeare.'

Without looking at her, I started in on a line. 'If I profane with my unworthiest hand this holy shrine' —I stopped, turned her to me, and watched her mouth as I spoke— 'the gentle sin is this: my lips, two blushing pilgrims, ready stand to smooth that rough touch with a tender kiss.'33

'Not too tender I hope.'

She kissed me, hard, and I took her by the hand again up the hill to my apartment.

The night morphed into morning and when we woke she kissed me and said she had to go. There were people who were expecting her. Borrowing from Booker, I told her sometimes people expect too much. She sighed dramatically, full of play and confidence, and said how true that was. Soon she was getting dressed and I watched her lovely nakedness disappear. Still in bed, I leaned on an elbow and told her I hoped to see her again. She smiled at me, blew me a kiss, and trilled a set of fingers over the same shoulder as she walked out the door.

·   ·   ·

The man on the balcony above Joe's Pizza, as you might have already guessed, was none other than the piss-ant himself, Grant Richards. His hands were stuck over the rail not to catch a ball, as it looked, but because he was filming me with his God damn cell phone. The fucker.

How do I know this? Emerson McKnight, buddy old pal that he is. And Emerson himself came by the information via a hand-ful of teachers who frequent his restaurant. The cloud-sniffing group of pedagogues who like to stroll into the upscale eatery, scarved even in June, with their standing Friday evening reserva-tion, and say things to their host like, 'Bon soir, Em-air-sohn,' even though there isn't a single crème de anything in the joint and all the wine they order is Ontarian.

I can just imagine their conversation:

'Oh, Emerson, we know you used to be acquainted with him, but really, he's a sad case.'

'A sad, sad case.'

'He's more than sad. He's a menace. An embarrassment.'

---

33 There's no way you would have let me get away with such a display.

'Yes, an embarrassment. That's what he is. An embarrassment. He's an embarrassment to our profession.'

'To our school.'

'To our community.'

'To the human race, if you'll pardon the hyperbole.'

'Yes, to the human race.'

'Can you imagine, a teacher selling dope to students.'

'To students!'

'Uhhchh. It's disgusting.'

'He's disgusting.'

'I hope I never lay eyes on him again.'

A moment goes by and Emerson enters the dialogue: 'I have to ask—are you absolutely certain that's what happened?'

'Oh, Emerson, don't be so naïve.'

'There's six—count them, six!—student testimonies.'

'Plus the video evidence.'

'No, there's no question he did it.'

'The truth is the truth. There's no denying that.'

'No, there certainly isn't.'

'You can't deny the truth.'

'No, you can't.'

'You can see him on the video plain as day.'

Emerson nods. 'So you've seen the video.'

'Well, yes, Emerson. We have.'

'Do you mind me asking what's on it exactly?'

'Oh, my, well, it's awful, just awful.'

'It is. Awful.'

'That slug of a man—'

'Yes, a slug.'

'—selling two marijuana cigarettes to one of our best and brightest students.'

'Don't worry though, he's been getting help.'

'Dean King, that is. The student.'

'Yes, he's doing much better.'

'Back on track, as they say.'

'You know that no good Dunn was actually his teacher?'

'Only for a month, thank heavens.'

'Still. A month of misanthropic misguidance.'

'Well put, well put.'

'Yes. Artfully articulated.'

'He's such an ogre.'

'Lecherous.'

'Uhhchh.'

'Indeed.'

'Disgusting, I agree.'

'Hey, did you know Dean was actually in the room when Mrs. Eckerton came in with the police and took Dunn away?'

One of them leans in. 'Should we be talking about this?'

'Oh, I think it's okay.'

'Sure it is.'

'It is. Go on.'

'Did Dean say anything?'

'Not a word.'

'Trying to protect the louse, no doubt.'

'Probably in shock, poor thing.'

'He looked up to him, you know.'

'A lot of them did.'

'Hard to believe.'

'He lured them with his lackadaisical teaching style.'

'Charmed them with his youth.'

'And his lies.'

'Brainwashed them.'

'Dreadful. Just dreadful.'

'A travesty is what it is.'

'Yes. A travesty.'

'To this day Dean defends that no good piece of you know what.'

'Poor thing.'

'One day he'll look back and see what a terrible influence Dunn was.'

'Sure, he'll be better for it in the end.'

'Experience is the best teacher, they say.'

'They do. And it is.'

'It is.'

'We all have our experiences, don't we?'

'We do.'

'Yes, we do.'

'Anyway.'

'Yes. Enough about him.'

'Uhhchh. What a waste.'

'We're sorry, Emerson. We know he was a friend of yours.'

'But you must be able to see now what a rotten seed he is.'

'It's hard to believe, I'm sure.'

Emerson sighs. 'You know, it is. It really is.'

Emerson, you turncoat.

'You think you know someone.'

'Yes, you do. I thought I did.'

You son-of-a-bitching backstabber, McKnight.

'But I do have to say, you've all piqued my curiosity.'

'Oh? How's that?'

'Well, again, you said you saw the video.'

'Yes. They made us watch it.'

'It was part of a PD session called Cleaning Up Our Community.'

'They brought the police in and everything.'

Emerson crosses his arms. 'Sounds interesting, very worthwhile.'

'Oh, it was, Emerson. It was.'

'Mm-hmn. Well, I was just wondering.'

'Yes?'

'I was just wondering if they talked about how the video came to be.'

Ah, Emerson, I take it all back. You devil. You sly, sly devil. You sleuth.

'Oh, well, yes, but we were told that in confidence.'

'And the police asked us not to discuss the session beyond the walls of the school.'

'Oh. Certainly. I understand.'

'But I do suppose it's okay if we tell you.'

'Sure it is. We can trust Emerson.'

'Yes, yes, of course we can.'

'You wouldn't say anything to anyone else.'

'Oh, no. Not a word. I'm just curious, seeing how he used to be a friend of mine.'

That a boy, Emerson. That a boy.

'Of course.'

'Yes. We understand.'

'Certainly. You have a right to know.'

'Well, only if you think it's okay.'

Nice. Make it their call. Well played, McKnight. Well played.

'You promise not to say anything?'

'Not a word.'

'Okay then. Here goes. You see, Grant Richards—one of our best and most respected English teachers—just so happened to be at his mother's apartment late one night at the end of August.'

'A Friday, I think.'

'Yes, I think so.'

'Anyway, she had phoned him around midnight.'

'Poor thing. She's confused.'

'Alzheimer's, I think.'

'Yes. I think so.'

'Right, well, she was having difficulty sleeping, couldn't find her pills or something.'

'We all have our troubles, don't we?'

'We do.'

'Anyway, good and doting son that he is, Grant got in his car and drove over to make sure she was alright.'

'He found her pills.'

'They were in the same spot they always were.'

'He stayed with her until she was able to fall asleep.'

'Such a good son.'

'He is.'

'Then he dozed a little himself in the armchair by her bed and woke up around three in the morning.'

'Yes, and then went out onto the balcony for a little fresh air.'

'Once he saw the time, he decided he might as well stay till morning.'

'Just to make sure his mother was okay.'

'Such a lovely man.'

'So lovely.'

'And when he was out there on the balcony he saw that sick, good-for-nothing Dunn come out of a bar across the road.'

'At three in the morning no less.'

'Uhhchh.'

'Figures. Low life that he is.'

'Anyway, Grant said he wasn't sure who it was at first, but then he heard someone up the street call out to Dunn.'

'It was Dean.'

'The student we told you about.'

'That's when Grant thought something was a little fishy and decided to pull his cell phone out just in case.'

'Good thing he did.'

'He could have been a detective, that man. I told him so, you know.'

'Yes. He could've been. I agree.'

'Anyway, he had an idea something was up.'

'So he started filming.'

'Nothing happened at first.'

'It looked like they were just talking.'

'You can see them plain as day on the video.'

'Dean and his two friends.'

'Dunn and some other scruffy-looking man.'

'Likely a junkie.'

'Grant zoomed right in on them.'

'You can see them talking.'

'And then it happens.'

'That filthy piece of refuse pulls two marijuana cigarettes from his back pocket and slips them to Dean.'

'Just like that.'

'Can you believe it?'

'Uhhchh.'

'Then Dean gives him the money and he puts it in his back pocket.'

'And there you have it.'

'All the evidence I need.'

'Case closed.'

'You can actually see him looking around to make sure no one saw.'

'The sneaky so-and-so.'

'Low life.'

'The lowest.'

'Yes, yes, but little did he know.'

'Ha ha, you said it.'

'Little did he know our saviour was perched right across the street.'

'Grant Richards, detective-teacher to the stars.'

'Isn't it just a blessing he was there when it happened?'

'It is. A blessing.'

'Just goes to show you. Good always prospers.'

'And evil never wins.'

'Amen to that.'

'Amen.'

'Amen.'

'Amen.'

'Makes you think how connected everything in the world is, though, doesn't it?'

'It does.'

'You know, Grant Richards is such a good man.'

'So put together.'

'So with it.'

'So intuitive.'

'To have the wherewithal and foresight to catch it all on film.'

'I don't know how he managed to stay so calm.'

'He's a gem of a man. We're lucky to have him.'

'As are the students.'

'Yes, the students.'

'Anyway, we've taken up enough of your time, Emerson.'

'Yes, listen to us, going on and on.'

'Babblers, gossipers, tongue-waggers are we.'

Group laughter.

'Not at all. I was the one to ask.'

'Oh, right. Yes.'

'Well, did we answer your question?'

'You did. You did. You've all been very helpful. What you said was very illuminating.'

'Illuminating. He's such an articulate man, isn't he?'

'He is. Very cultured.'

'Yes, cultured.'

'He is.'

'Anyway, on to happier topics.'

'Yes.'

'Agreed.'

'So, how's that lovely wife of yours?'

'Lovely as always.'

'Oh, you're such a dear. He's such a dear.'

'Such a sweetheart.'

'A sweetheart, yes.'

'A darling of a man.'

'A darling.'

Uhhchh.

'So, my darling, Em-air-sohn, I've been dying to ask you. Did you manage to acquire some of that Late Autumn Reisling I mentioned last week?'

'I did.'

'Oh goodie. We'll take a bottle to start.'

'I've had one chilling all afternoon in anticipation of your arrival.'

Emerson, the restaurateur, the politician.

'And when you get to the bottom of the first, there's more in the back.'

They'd have at least a bottle each by the time the evening was through, I'm sure.

'Oh, you're naughty, Mr. McKnight.'

'Naughty but nice.'

'Nice and naughty.'

Giggle, giggle, giggle.

I don't know how he stood them. But he did and I was ever grateful. I felt all the more justified in seeking my revenge once I had the details of Richards' little documentary. I did wonder, though, how my good friend rationalized his duplicitous and irreligious snooping with respect to his newly found faith. When I asked, he explained that the loyalty he felt towards me outweighed the betrayal of the teachers at his restaurant. So he was okay. As far as he saw it, lying for the sake of fidelity was a perfectly Catholic thing to do. I wouldn't know. But whatever makes him rest easy. He's a hell of a friend.

Now, in keeping with my own efforts towards honesty, I should mention that I have taken a few liberties with the dialogue in my retelling-slash-imagining of the little Emerson-teacher episode transcribed above. I did so mostly in an attempt to draw an honest portrait of the group of oh-so-forthcoming ex-colleagues of mine whose names I've respectfully kept undisclosed (I don't need any lawsuits), although I'm sure they'd recognize themselves should they ever have occasion to read these pages. (*Aside.* Of course, should a reader ever recognize himself in anything he reads, the bulk of the blame goes to him, not to the writer.) Retelling-slash-imagining aside, the nuts and bolts of the exchange are essentially true and accurate.

Another problem with truth: accuracy.

So. Now you know the details of the night that changed my life. I'll let you, dear reader, be the judge.[34]

.   .   .

As for formal charges, Eckleburg and the Board representatives were politely told that they did not have nearly enough evidence against me to make anything—other than maybe Possession—stick in court. Richards' little documentary was, according to the powers that be, 'inconclusive,' and the six so-called testimonies Eckleburg had managed to rally against me were all from students with personal vendettas who had failed classes of mine and could easily be shown, through a well drawn defence, to have ulterior motives. Although I managed with ease to elude any fines, community service, or jail time (in

---

[34] And you, Aislinn. I'll let you be the judge.

this situation, at least), the Board members assured me that from their point of view there was ample evidence to have me brought before the School Board Disciplinary Committee. Which they did. And rather swiftly.

So, to the SBDC I went, with little hope in tow and my reputation already in ruins. The proceedings that followed saw me charged and summarily convicted of trafficking marijuana to students. I was promptly relieved of my position with the Board and my teaching license was revoked, a pronouncement permanently stamped beside my name on the publicly accessible, easily navigable College of Teachers website, not to mention the spot I earned within the inglorious blue pages of the monthly College magazine where my case was given a detailed and defamatory little write-up. A solid bit of inter-office and dinner table conversation fodder for teachers around the province, no doubt. And as though this spot of infamy weren't enough, the Heron River Review, one of two local rags, ran a typically ungrammatical (some solace at least) front-page article on my shameful debauchery and decline. The piece, stupidly titled 'Dunn Deserves the Dungeon,' was written by one of the establishment's tenured and most senior Neanderthals, accompanied, somehow, by a photograph of my handcuffed and blubbering removal from the school.

I include verbatim the final 'sentence' of the article here for a sample, journalistic gem that it is: 'There's no room—no room at all at any of our Inns, we say, with our furious and fulminating fists slamming down—for a so-called man such as the sin-ridden Benjamin Fred Dunn to amble about and walk up and down the streets of our morally upstanding town as he pleases (because, let me reiterate, it does not please us), and not to mention there is no place for him in the classrooms of higher—not lower!—learning in our one and only academic high school where he can continue to damage the young minds and character of our young people and children who are the very future of this town, Heron River, and the world, for that matter, not to mention for what we all stand for, which, for one thing for certain, will not be the likes of one Ben Fredrick Dunne, but will instead be what we all believe in: Goodness, Ethicalness and Honestness.'

Petty of me to include this, I know. But really, if there is to be any talk of wrongdoing, so-called sin, or even crime, it should begin in places like the HRR. Such abuse of language, like any other act of cruelty, should not be tolerated.

So. To the revenge. After my little chat with Booker the morning we checked out of the St. John's pen, I bought a ticket to Toronto and flew out the very next day. My co-conspirator and all around mastermind saw me off—plan in hand—with a smirking 'God spede' on his lips.

When I got to Toronto I called Vicky Fern, a 'close and very dear actor friend' of Booker's. Her actual name, she told me, was Victoria Ferenghetti. She had changed it for the stage, which had worked out very well so far. I had yet to say more than my own name when I learned that Vicky was currently playing Ariel in a Survivor interpretation of The Tempest for an upstart, experimental theatre company called Under the Sun. How the show worked, she told me, was each act began with an unscripted challenge called The Shakespeare Shakedown—which included categories like *Who Said It?*, *Mime the Rhyme*, and *Kill Bill* (questions dedicated to Shakespeare's murderers)—giving the actors a chance to earn immunity (Propsero's staff doubled as the idol), and at the end of each act, the audience voted off their least favourite character. They even had tribal council with a Shakespeare-garbed, sonneteering Jeff-Probst-type host leading the way. What Vicky liked about the production most, she explained, was the collaborative improvisation that it took to get through each scene with successively fewer actors. As a side note, she was quite proud of the fact that after three weeks and ten shows, Ariel had yet to be voted off.

'Something to put on your CV,' I said.

'It's already there. Winner of the Audience Award for Best Loved Performer during Under the Sun's '09 Fall season.'

We were going to get along just fine. I could tell.

At the end of our conversation we arranged to meet at Bon Hommes, one of the innocuously named gay bars on Church Street, only a minute's walk from her basement apartment on

Wellesley. After discussing the details of the part she'd play in my little revenge plot, we decided that Bon Hommes would be the perfect place to arrange to meet Richards for her interview with him in her role as junior *Globe & Mail* journalist Patricia Duncan. She was new to the job, she'd tell him, but eager and thrilled to be doing a story on a Governor General's Award winner as one of her first assignments.

Before hanging up I asked her how I'd know who she was.

'I'll be the one with the pink streak in my otherwise midnight black hair. I'll be wearing throwback Doc Martens laced to the knee. I'll have on pink-framed fifties-style glasses. I'll be in a booth at the back. There will be a pack of Cameos on the table. I'll point when I see you coming and I'll call out your name. How's that?'

'I can't imagine missing you.'

'Oh, you will.'

'I meant—'

Dial tone. She was gone. I took a cab and walked into Bon Hommes about ten minutes later.

It was six o'clock. Shift change. The place was nearly empty. I saw her right away—impossible to miss—and walked towards her. She pointed and called out my name, louder than I expected.

'Ben Dunn!'

We shook hands and I sat. I liked her right away. She was smart, spunky, quick, and from what little I'd seen and heard so far, skilled at her craft. Skipping all small talk, we moved right into discussing the plan and Patricia Duncan's 'motivation,' after which she slipped seamlessly into her role and used me as a Richards stand-in.

'Mr. Richards, I do have to say, it is a privilege to meet such an accomplished teacher. It is plain to see from what the jurors have written—praise in the highest degree—just how extraordinary an educator you really are. The selfless hours you put in, your professorial knowledge of Language and Literature, your innovative and highly effective pedagogy, your commitment to both school and community, your undying patience, your professionalism, the individual attention you give so many of your students. The superlatives are nearly endless for the work you have done, and continue to do, day in and day out. You counter with ease the all-too-common public perception of the indolent, self-serving, whiny teacher. You are a testament to a dying breed, Mr. Richards. The consummate, archetypal pedagogue. The gracious sage on the mount who, rather than forcing his would-be students to clamber their way up to him, comes humbly down, of his own accord, to greet his learners on a common, accessible level. You are a bastion of hope, a flagship for your profession. If only your fervour and facility of craft were something as easily transferable to the next generation of teachers as this award has been, so deservingly, to you. I dare say that if there were more people like you on the other side of the desk, the future of education would not, as the pundits predict, be an endangered world, but a secure, highly effectual, productive, self-sustaining, and ever-blooming one, redolent with possibility.

'Now, if you'll only bear with me, Mr. Richards. I have so many questions I want to get to. First, I know the readers of this article will want to know what brought you to teaching. Was it a calling? I mean did you always know you wanted to help develop the minds and shape the collective character of our nation's youth? What is it that motivates you to roll up your sleeves and dig into your work every day? What gives you satisfaction? What makes you tick? What does it mean to be Grant Richards?'

She was perfect. I grinned, leaned back, and folded my arms. 'Unbelievable.'

She threw her hands up and nearly lunged across the table.

'Unbelievable? You wouldn't know believable if a God damn fairy drove a wand up your ass and tickled your innards. What you just witnessed was stage worthy. Pure dramatic gold. And if you can't see that you can go pan up Shit River, for all I care, and lick the sediment that settles in your sifter. Mister.'

Just as quickly as she had climbed across the table, she sat back and examined a thumbnail while pontificating on the necessity of range and the ability to switch moods in an instant.

'An irate, comically hysterical actor is an essential character for any thespian to have in her arsenal. What'd you think of mine?'

I nodded. 'Bang on. I didn't know whether to laugh or look over my shoulder for the exit.'

She leaned across the table, took my hands, and stared at me longingly. Her voice softened—her eyes began to well. 'Oh, Ben, please. You can't leave. You just can't. I don't know what I'd do. You're my life. You're everything to me. Oh, stay with me, Ben. Stay with me. I'll make you happy. I promise. You'll see. Don't leave, Ben. Please. I can't do it without you. I can't do it alone.'

She was weeping by the end of it. As genuine a display as I'd ever seen, real or otherwise.

'Jesus—you are good.'

She used both hands to wipe her face, took a deep breath, and looked right at me. 'You should see me in bed.'

She tongued the soft curve of her upper lip. I'm sure my mouth fell open. She smirked and fell back against the cushioned booth.

A few moments passed. She looked about the place. There was someone behind the bar but no waiters were visible on the floor. I cleared my throat.

'So where did you say you knew Booker from again?'

She lit one of the Cameos and blew smoke across the table. 'I didn't.'

'Right. You didn't.'

'Does it matter?'

'No, not at all. I was just curious.'

I scratched at a bubble in the finish of the table.

'About what?'

I pressed my lips together, shrugged.

'You want to know if we were in love.' She exaggerated the phrase *in love*, drew on her cigarette again, and exhaled. 'Or if we were fuck buddies.'

'It's none of my business. Really.'

'So why did you ask?'

'I didn't.'

'Right,' she smirked. 'You didn't.'

She drew on her cigarette a third and final time before blotting it out on the underside of the table and returning it to the package.

'Maybe he pays me.'

She was looking at me now and she waited until I looked at her. When I did, she leaned back and slipped her right hand down the front of her pants.

'Maybe you want to pay me.'

She closed her eyes, moved her hand up and down, and moaned. I whipped my head over both shoulders and leaned across the table.

'Jesus Christ, what're you doing? What's wrong with you?'

She continued—moving her hand, moaning—and then, like a flicked switch, she stopped, opened her eyes, reached out, and honked my nose.

'Got you again.'

I fell back against my side of the booth. 'Jesus. You are something.'

'How precise of you.'

I sighed, clasped my hands behind my head, and stretched my legs under the table. She mimicked me. Our feet touched. Neither of us drew away.

I grinned. 'Let's have a drink, Vicky Fern.'

'Let's.'

She caught the attention of the first waiter I'd seen since arriving. A well groomed twenty-something lover of men who, genuinely excited to see her, took her by the shoulders when she stood and kissed both her cheeks.

'Gregory J,' he announced, extending a manicured hand, and I noticed the nametag on his fitted sweater which confirmed what he'd said.

When I told him who I was, Gregory J made a revelatory sort of gasp, pointed, and spoke with the kind of intonation I expected. 'Oh, I know you.'

I looked at Vicky, then at Gregory J. 'No, I don't think you do.'

'Sure, sure. You're the singer.'

Shit. The YouTube video from The Rose & Thistle. Christ.

'Oh, well, listen. That wasn't my most dignified moment.'

'What do you mean?'

'The video you saw. That wasn't me at my best.'

'What video?'

I shook my head. 'Never mind.'

Leaning forward, Vicky lowered her glasses and peered at me over the rims. 'No, no, no. Always mind. Always mind. But before we get to this video you speak of' —she turned to Gregory J— 'why don't you tell Mr. Dunn how you knew he was a singer.'

She was prodding. I could tell. I just couldn't tell why.

Gregory J blushed. He looked everywhere but at me. 'Okay. Well. This may make you a little uncomfortable. So I apologize if it does. But the thing is—oh, this is embarrassing.' He touched his lips with an index finger, gathered himself, and continued. 'Oh, shit, I'll just say it. Here goes. I *know*—I mean I guess it's more accurate to say I *knew*—a good friend of yours very well. I mean *very* well.'

I waited. He sighed, tilted his head.

'Wyatt Stone. He had my heart.'

You've got to be kidding me.

'We used to be quite the group about town. Wyatt and I would meet up with Vicky and—oh, who's that cute clever quirky guy who used to come visit you all the time?'

'Booker.'

Gregory J looked at me, a little surprised. 'Yeah, Booker. You know him, too?'

'Yes. I know him, too.'

Vicky touched my hand. I looked at her. She was grinning. Booker must have told her about my connection to Wyatt. She was testing me. I could tell.

'Oh, right, right, right. He was part of the band. The River Bank.'

'Edge.'

'Hmn?'

'The River's Edge.'

'Oh, yes. Silly me.' He looked at Vicky. 'What was that, Vick, three, four years ago?'

She nodded, still grinning, and said nothing.

'Mmmm, I remember those days—come to think of it, Wyatt wasn't even out yet.' Gregory J giggled and touched my shoulder. 'The closeted ones are always the most fun.'

I furrowed my brow, folded and unfolded my arms, and looked at the hand he'd placed on my shoulder. He noticed me looking, withdrew the hand, and batted the air.

'Oh, don't worry, I didn't mean you, Benjamin. I can tell if a guy has potential quicker than vodka makes Vicky here strip to her panties and dance on tables.'

The two of them laughed. I could feel my face tighten. He tsked. Apparently both my discomfort and displeasure thickened the air around me.

'Look, Benjamin, don't flatter yourself. There's no need for you to sit there all puckered up and sour-faced. I knew you were straight as soon as I shook your hand. A firm assertion of your hetero status. Impressive. If you'd squeezed any harder I might have squealed.'

I didn't know whether to feel reassured or insulted.

He folded his arms. 'Wyatt used to talk about you. A lot. It killed him not being able to tell you. He was terrified what you'd think.'

I nodded. 'Was he really.'

'He was. Terrified.'

'And he told you this?'

'He told me everything back then.'

I folded my arms, looked up at him, and nodded. His eyes popped and he covered his mouth with his fingers.

'Oh, shit. Please tell me you knew.' He checked with Vicky. 'I mean, he's his best friend. How could he not have told his best friend by now?'

Yes, Gregory J was good, too, I thought. Another actor plying his craft at my expense. Maybe Vicky had recruited him to be the other key player in my little revenge plot. Maybe he wanted to show me his wares.

I stopped him with a hand. 'Okay, okay.'

Gregory J looked confused.

'Listen, you're very good.'

'What are you talking about? Good at what?'

He looked at Vicky, his face all screwed up with confusion.

'Forget it. And don't worry. Wyatt told me.'

He mimed wiping sweat from his brow. 'Phew.'

'Three months ago.'

'Shit. You're kidding. It took him that long?'

I nodded.

'Well, you know, it doesn't really surprise me.'

'Why do you say that?'

'I'm sure you can see it. Wyatt's as straight as gay guys come. His type are always the last to come out.'

For some reason I felt relieved by this.

Gregory J touched his chin. 'You know, I really do think about him a lot.' He sighed again, tilted his head. 'Like I said, he had my heart.'

Vicky cut in. 'Speaking of hearts, what do say to a Bloody Mary, Ben? The boys here at Bon Hommes make the best in the city.'

Thank you, Vicky.

Gregory J took the pencil from his ear and started writing.

'I'll bring you a plate of our bruschetta. To die for. Really. Ooh, and some calamari.'

I nodded and continued to nod as I spoke. 'And a double of JD each. And two pints of something dark.' I handed Gregory J my credit card. 'That should do to start.'

'Ooh, someone's in the mood to party.'

I was still nodding. Gregory J raised his brow at Vicky who raised hers in return.

'Don't worry. I'll be quick as a bunny.'

He turned and actually hopped twice before slipping into the kind of stride I expected. I closed my eyes. Vicky tapped the table.

'You don't like it here, do you?'

I looked at her and played dumb. 'Here? Well, I was in Ireland for a while, then St. John's. Tough to beat places like that.'

'You know what I mean. Here. This bar. This environment.'

'It's fine. A bar's a bar. I'm just not used to being in one this long without a drink.'

I picked up the menu and pretended to leaf through it.

'Yes. But this is a gay bar.'

'Gay bar, shmay bar. What's the difference?'

'I think it's pretty clear. Gay bars attract, you know, gay people. This one, in particular, attracts gay men.'

I snapped the menu shut, furrowed my brow. 'So what are you saying?'

'I'm saying you fear queer. You nay gay. In short, you're a brow-protruding homophobe.'

'Listen. You don't know me.'

'I know enough.'

'Really.'

'You don't think I'd ask Booker why a friend of his wants me to arrange to meet some teacher in a gay bar and pretend to interview him about some fake award he's won while said friend sits in cognito a few tables away, video camera in hand, waiting for me to excuse myself so that a flamboyantly gay friend of mine can swoop in and unabashedly hit on the unsuspecting award-winning teacher, pretending to know him from previous nights of mutual pleasure, all loud and visually provocative enough for your little espionage film project?'

'So you do have someone for the other part.'

'Jesus. You're incorrigible.'

'You don't hear many people use that word anymore. It suits you.'

She shook her head. 'I would never have guessed you as one of Booker's friends.'

That hurt.

'I'm sorry. It's just I get so excited when I think of the whole thing coming together. You have no idea.'

'You're right. I don't.'

'You said you asked Booker.'

'I did. He didn't tell me.'

'So you really don't know anything. About why I'm doing this, I mean.'

'No. I don't. All he said when I asked was, *Victoria, my dear, purpose reveals itself through action.*'

Good old Booker.

Gregory J came swooping in with a tray of drinks and two plates of food. He set it all out expertly and asked if there would be anything else. I told him everything was perfect. Absolutely perfect. I raised my double Jack Daniel's to him, then to Vicky, and motioned for her to pick the other one up. She waved it off and cradled one of the Bloody Marys in her fingers. I handed the other Jack to Gregory J and told him I wouldn't take no for an answer.

'I can't. Really. I could get in trouble.'

I looked at him. He made a flourish of his hands and laughed. 'Oh, what the hell.'

He sat beside Vicky and I made a toast. 'To the sweetest nectar life has to offer.'

We all clinked glasses and I muttered a single word under my breath: *revenge*.

Gregory J and I drank to the bottom of our glasses and tabled them. He closed his eyes, puckered his lips, and shook his head. I picked up one of the pints, clinked Vicky's Bloody Mary, and continued to drink.

'Savour the heat, Gregory J. Savour the heat.'

He gave a full body shiver, stood, and thanked me for the drink. I nodded and lifted my pint towards him as he left.

'You know, he's not so bad. He's a good guy really.'

'You sound like you're having a revelation, Ben Dunn.'

I looked at her and drank. 'I don't believe in revelations. True understanding takes time.'

Smirking, she nodded. 'I understand.'

The moment passed. Vicky sipped her Bloody Mary and I looked away from the table. It was our first stretch of silence in a while. Then, not aggressively, I turned back to her.

'You know what? So what if I'm a homophobe? Is that some kind of sin?'

'I don't know if it's a sin. Maybe to a Christian homosexual. But it does make you a boor.'

I nodded. 'A boor. Yes, that's exactly what I am. A boor.'

'You say that like you're proud of it.'

I held my pint up and stared at it as though it were some ancient chalice holding the elixir of eternal life. I swallowed the remaining half of the pint in a trilogy of successive gulps, wiped my mouth with my sleeve, and touched my chest with a fist.

'Vicky, dear' —I did my best to mute a belch— 'I'm not proud of anything.'

I was good and drunk by the time we left Bon Hommes, but not raucously drunk. I had managed to remain relatively quiet and conversational throughout the evening. I hadn't made a spectacle of myself. No one other than Vicky Fern and Gregory J would remember me from that night. There had been no video recording of the two or three JDs and dozen or so pints, which was good. I needed to be able to slip back into that place unnoticed come the night of my little play.

Vicky and I left the bar around midnight and she offered me the couch in her basement apartment. Getting me down the stairs took some effort, I'm sure. I slept past noon the next day. I woke to the smell of coffee, toast, and eggs. I staggered into the kitchen and found Vicky wrapping an egg sandwich and pouring a hangover's worth of black coffee into a mug with a lid.

'Good morning.' She looked at the clock. 'I mean afternoon.'

She smiled and tapped me on the head.

I squeezed my eyes shut. 'Yes, well, good's a relative term, isn't it.'

She moved to the bottom of the stairs that connected her underground life to the world above and held out the coffee and bagged sandwich the way stationed volunteers hold out cups of water to marathoners passing by. I took my cue. And my breakfast. She followed me up the stairs and out of her apartment. It was cold, but there was no wind and the late morning sky was storybook blue. The sun was high and bright. She stood there, squinting, rubbing her shoulders.

I thanked her for the breakfast and the couch, told her I'd be in touch. She looked around, ran a hand through her hair. 'I'm sorry for some of what I said last night.'

'Don't be. It's me who should be sorry.'

(*Aside.* If only I could go back and erase all the 'shoulds' from my life.)

She looked down, etched a half-moon in the snow with her slipper.

'Oh—I nearly forgot.'

I removed one of my gloves and pulled my wallet from the inside of my jacket, counted out two-fifty, folded the bills, and handed them to her. I imagined Richards on a balcony nearby, arms outstretched, cell-phone-recording what he thought was another seedy transaction.

'I'll give you the rest the night of our little play.'

She looked at the fold, nodded, and tucked it inside her over-sized sweater. 'Thanks.'

'And here's your friend's half.'

I counted out and gave her another two-fifty.

'I'll be sure he gets it.'

She looked over her shoulder, down at the half-moon in the snow, then at me again. I looked down the street, checked my watch, and batted my gloved palms together.

'I guess I should go. The well-travelled road awaits.'

'You should take the one less travelled by.'

'You're right. I should. But I never do.'

'Which, if I had to bet, has made all the difference.'

'More than you can imagine.'

She shrugged. 'We can't all be heroes.'

'No, we can't. The world needs a bum or two.'

Hugging herself, she turned to go. I watched her. She opened the door and looked over her shoulder. 'For what it's worth, I don't think you're a bum.'

She turned and the door closed behind her. I breathed the cold air deeply in and headed for Church, kicking bits of snow as I went, gloved hands drawn behind my back as though cuffed. An honest, impish little grin smeared across my face.

I took a cab to Union Station and bought a ticket home. I was reluctant, to say the least, but I had to go. There were things I needed to take care of, things that were long overdue.

Regardless of what anyone knew of my career-ending debacle, I was sure to encounter very few fans of Ben Frederick Dunn, biological but certainly not worthy son of the late Walter Dunn. My hometown was the type of place neighbours quietly kept track of how often you visited your parents, secretly judged how good a son you were based on their own set of credentials. A man who doesn't even attend his own father's funeral is quickly determined to be wholly unworthy of any sympathy, respect, or consideration he might otherwise have coming to him as a member—however distant he's become geographically—of a small, tightly woven community such as Castorville. I deserved to be shunned. It's what I expected.

The ticket took me as far as Oshawa on the train and included a transfer for the bus that would ferry me the rest of the way home. I sat in the back, hunkered down, hiding behind the novel *Joshua, Then and Now* (I remember feeling like Kevin Hornby, both of us responsible for particular and irreparable rents in the fabric of the places we were from). I thought if I tried hard enough I could slip into town unnoticed, quietly take care of what I needed to take care of, and slip out again like an undetected marauder in the night.

After the bus had made its penultimate stop, only five passengers remained. I recognized none of them and it was clear none of them knew me. I was relieved but somewhat disappointed. Part of me had hoped to be recognized, to be welcomed home despite the many disgraces that preceded me. The way some people adamantly refuse to believe the stories of condemnation about a certain family member, and instead of spurning said member greet him upon his return, unquestioningly, with open arms.

The bus let the five of us off at the corner of Main and Simcoe. Everyone but me was met by someone waiting in a car. Soon I was alone. It was Sunday, just after the dinner hour, already dark at this time in December. The light posts were decorated with garland and fake oversized candles that remained lit throughout the night. Otherwise, the street showed no signs of life. The stores were all closed and everyone was at home. I zipped my jacket, flipped the hood, pocketed my gloved hands, and headed over the bridge toward Railway Street, aptly named for its location parallel to the tracks. At the end of the street stood the house I'd grown up in. It was where I'd yelled at my father the last time I'd seen him, where I could picture him perched in his armchair in the living room, staring blankly at the muted TV, an old photograph of *her* in his lap, alive only in his waiting. In truth, I half expected him to be there when I dropped my backpack, took the key from under the large stone by the porch, and opened the door.

He wasn't of course. The house was empty. As empty a place as I'd ever been. I wanted to leave as soon as I entered. I could hear the fridge running, and for some reason the radio had been left on, quiet and distant. It was cold standing there in the kitchen. There was the scent of him still—the musk of his work clothes, the ghost of steeped tea—and I could see my breath in the darkness of the place I'd once called home.

Though he hadn't had a drink in years (except the mouthful of beer he choked down on my account the last time I saw him), my father always kept a bottle in the cupboard above the fridge so he could offer visitors something stronger than tea when they arrived. I say 'visitors,' but really there was only one. Besides the odd time I showed up, the only other person my father had contact with outside of work was his next-door neighbour, Bill Jeffrey, a man who had worked with the Motors for thirty-two years and was now five years into retirement. He was yet to turn sixty. His wife, Laura, also in her fifties, ran Laura's Tea Room in town, something she had always dreamed of doing. When their two daughters, Kris and Sarah, were finished school and making their own way in the world, she and Bill 'found the perfect little spot and made it happen,' as he said. True to his generation, Bill had been good with his money and after helping his daughters through university there was still enough left to get the Tea Room off the ground. A cozy little corner shop on Main Street, it attracted a regular group of locals, mostly retirees, and during the summer months many of the city cottagers stopped by for their morning coffee and daily dose of small-town hospitality. The pies and tarts and other pastries Laura sold were baked at home every Wednesday evening and Sunday afternoon, a ritual she looked forward to and enjoyed as much as pulling the blinds and flipping the Open sign every morning at seven. It was during one of these baking sessions that Bill would visit my father. Every week. Until he didn't.

And so I'm sure it was strange for Bill Jeffrey to be tromping up the porch steps to Walter Dunn's front door the morning after I arrived.

He knocked and waited, then knocked again. I'm not sure how long it took for the knocking to wake me, but when I finally pushed my weary, heavy-headed self from my father's armchair and shuffled to the front door, Bill's nose had gone red in the cold and the hand he offered when I opened the door was freezing when I shook it.

'Ben.'

'Mr. Jeffrey.'

We had never really said much more than hello to each other. There had never been a weekend of fishing for the Dunn and Jeffrey men. No games of football or catch spanning our back-yards, no shared Hockey Night in Canada. I'd never had that type of relationship with my father and Bill had never had a son. Although we were neighbours for nearly twenty years before I left for university, Mr. Jeffrey and I were essentially strangers.

'Just dropped Laura at the shop there and saw the prints in the snow. Figured it must be you.'

I nodded, hungover, still not fully awake.

'Thought we'd see you long before now.'

I nodded again, hugged myself, rubbed my arms.

The wind blew. Swirls of snow lifted in the driveway, like dust, and settled.

'Sorry. I'm standing here letting the winter in.'

I shook my head, which hurt, stepped to the side, and ges-tured for him to enter. He followed me to the kitchen table and took what I assumed to be his regular seat. He looked around the place like it was his childhood home and he'd come back after forty years to see how much or how little it had changed since the days he resided there.

I went to the washroom off the kitchen, ran the water cold, splashed my face, leaned heavily on the counter with both hands and assessed the mug looking back at me in the mirror: a week of no shaving, dark puffy bags below my eyes, the beginnings of per-manent curves from the corners of my mouth to the edges of my nose, creases across my forehead, a rogue silver hair in the return-ing shagginess of the mop on my head. I could see myself at fifty.

I sighed and took a hand towel from the cupboard by the sink, buried my face in it, and tried to wipe away what I'd just seen in the mirror. I held the towel there, pressed it against my face, and inhaled.

I hadn't expected the smell. Unlike the trace that lingered in the rest of the house, there was the fullness of him infused in the soft fabric of the towel. Like he was right there. Like we were hugging hello or goodbye, which we never did. I held the towel in one hand like it was a skull and looked at it, considered how something that no longer existed could seem so real.

I returned to the kitchen a little more awake and sat across from Mr. Jeffrey.

'Coffee?'

He nodded. 'I'd drink a coffee.'

I scanned the cupboards from my chair. 'Do you know if he has . . . if he had a—'

'I don't think so. He always drank tea.'

I know that, I thought. I know my father always drank tea.

I stood and went through the cupboards, found a jar of instant coffee. 'This okay?'

He nodded. I found two mugs, spooned the crystals in. Filled the kettle, set it on the stove. I sort of pushed on the table as I lowered myself into the chair. My head pounded.

'Heard you went to Ireland.'

I nodded.

'Supposed to be beautiful.'

'It is.'

Although I didn't really know Mr. Jeffrey, I understood the way people in general spoke around here. He would never tell me he'd heard why I hadn't been at the funeral, and if he knew, he'd never say anything directly about what had happened in Heron River.

'My youngest—you know Sarah—she's a teacher too.'

There it was. He knew.

'Science and math. Beyond me. Always was a smart one, that girl. Said she seen you at some teacher conference or something.'

I remembered. We were at one of those mandatory PD sessions at the Board office. We kept looking at each other, furtively, trying to confirm whether who each of us saw was who we thought we saw. Sarah was five or six years older than me, which put her sister, Kris, seven or eight years older. Because they were girls and because of the age gap between us, I'd talked to them even less than I'd talked to their father. Growing up, there might as well have been four adults next door.

'They make you go to those things. Waste of time really.'

'Sarah says the same.'

I nodded. He knew that I knew he knew. I could tell.

The kettle boiled and I made the coffee. 'Milk or sugar?'

'Milk if there's any.'

It had been too long to trust anything in the fridge. Without having to think I went to the utensils drawer, took out a spoon and a can opener. I opened the cupboard directly beneath the drawer and found a can of condensed milk. Strange the things that remain automatic.

The coffee was strong and bitter. You could tell it was instant, but it did the job. I snapped my fingers and left the table, returned with the bottle I'd rescued from the cupboard above the fridge the night before.

'A little early in the day, I know, but all things considered.'

Not wanting to see the paternal look of disapproval I assumed Mr. Jeffrey would have on his face, I poured a healthy shot into my mug before offering him the bottle. To my surprise he took it and poured himself a similar amount.

'All things considered,' he said.

We raised our mugs to the empty space between us and drank.

We didn't talk much for the first little bit. When we got to the bottom of our mugs I rose and made more coffee. We passed the can of milk and the bottle between us again. Soon my headache was gone and the warmth was running through me.

I hadn't planned on asking anyone for help, but now that I was here I realized I couldn't do the things I needed to do on my own. I also realized that my father's long time neighbour and friend was the only person I could ask.

'Mr. Jeffrey?'

'Bill. Please.'

I felt strange calling him by his first name.

'I know this is probably out of line, but I was wondering if I could ask you a favour.'

He folded his hands on the table and looked at me.

'I thought I'd sell the house.'

He nodded.

'It's just, I can't live here.'

'No.'

By the way he said 'no,' I knew he meant he understood *why* I couldn't live there.

'And I can't just leave it abandoned.'

'No.'

Again, his 'no' meant more than 'no.'

I leaned back in the chair, hands clasped behind my head. 'It's not that I need the money.'

He ran a thumbnail through a crack in the table and shook his head.

'Others will think that,' I said.

He shrugged. 'People will think what they think. There's no stopping them.'

It was something Norman Scott would've said.

I sat forward, leaned my forearms on the table. 'The thing is, I don't know how to go about it. I've never sold a house before.'

He drained his mug and looked at it. 'Can't say I have either.'

He'd lived next door his whole adult life.

I got up and made us each one more coffee. The end of the crystals.

I spoke over my shoulder. 'Can't be too hard though.'

'No. Can't imagine.'

I handed him his coffee and sat. We forewent the condensed milk and shared the bottle once more. I looked at the clock above the sink. Not yet eight.

'I'll call Jim Jones later this morning.'

'Jim Jones. I know that name.'

'Runs the Real Estate in town. Has for thirty years. Had a son about your age.'

My eyes narrowed. I nodded. 'Yeah, yeah. I remember. Jimmy Jones. He still around?'

Besides Wyatt, the people I'd grown up with in Castorville were like characters in a book on a shelf I couldn't reach. There, but not. All but forgotten.

'He was killed a few winters ago. Snowmobile accident. Ran clear into an ice hut. Two in the morning. Well into his cups, I'm sure. But that was only a rumour. Nothing official. The real problem was the hut was way off by itself, no reflectors. Hit it straight on going over a hundred. Blew the hut to pieces. Dead on impact.'

'Jesus.'

He nodded. 'Yep.'

'I hadn't heard.'

He could've easily said something like, *How would you have heard? You're one of those his-shit-doesn't-stink, holier-than-thou little fuckers who leaves and never looks back. You barely even visited your own father. You didn't even come to his funeral for Christ sake. Some son. Honestly, I don't know how you look at yourself in the mirror.*

But he didn't say anything like this. In fact, he didn't say anything at all. Instead he tipped his mug and finished the third coffee. I did the same. They were becoming much easier to drink. We set our mugs on the table. I looked over at the counter where the empty jar of crystals sat.

'We're out of coffee.'

He nodded.

I grabbed the bottle by its neck and poured half of what was left into my mug. 'Might as well finish this off too.'

There was enough for a healthy double each. Mr. Jeffrey held his mug out for his share and I drained the bottle into it.

'All things considered.'

I nodded. 'All things considered.'

.   .   .

'Once I finished up at the Motors we opened up Laura's Tea Room and I took to woodworking. Something I always had a love for but no time.'

We were in Mr. Jeffrey's garage which looked like a high school wood shop on a smaller scale. The only difference was the

bar fridge in one corner next to the metal table with two chairs.
A radio and a folded newspaper sat on the table. Everything else,
organized and uncluttered, was wood and tools.

He went to the fridge and without asking handed me a beer.

'This here's a cradle I'm working on.'

He ran a hand down the smooth length of wood held within a vice.

'A grandfather. Jesus.' He shook his head. 'Where the time
goes.'

I didn't know what to say. I drank the beer. It was cold and
good.

He walked me around the garage explaining what certain
tools were for. I nodded at the names like I knew what everything was and how it all worked when really I'd never sawed or
planed a piece of wood in my life. I'd scarcely driven a nail to
hang a picture. To my generation, a router was something you
needed to get online.

'Ah. Here it is.' He set his beer down on a nearby worktable
and touched the top of a canvas tarp draped over what I assumed
to be one of his projects. 'This is what I wanted to show you.'

He took a corner of the tarp and unveiled the rocking chair
beneath.

'Just this last year I convinced him to come over and tinker
around. He mentioned one time how he'd enjoyed it in school.'

I took the top of the chair in one hand and rocked it back
and forth.

'He was pretty near done. Some sanding, I think. Couple
coats of varnish.'

It was difficult for me to picture my father in here, working
the tools, cutting and shaping lengths of wood, meticulously piec-
ing together the bones of this rocking chair.

'I had no idea.'

'He was good. A natural. Never had to be told how to do
something. Just did it.'

I looked at Mr. Jeffrey, asking without words if it was okay if
I sat. He nodded and so I did. I held the arms and rocked back and
forth. As I did, I thought of my father doing the same, rocking in

this chair he'd built himself, a cup of tea nearby, the trace of a smile on his face.

'That day, you know, I was going over to ask him if he wanted to go into business with me. Nothing serious. Take a few orders. Put a few pieces in Laura's Tea Room. Give us both something to work towards. He only had a month or two left at the factory. Would've been a good way for him to put in the time. Good as any I suppose.'

I nodded even though my father's imminent retirement was news to me.

'You know, I haven't told this to anyone. Not even Laura. Maybe it's the coffee talking. Maybe it's because you're his son. I don't know. Thing is, something just felt different that day. May sound silly, but walking up those porch steps I sensed something in the air. Kind of like—I don't know—his spirit or something. I knocked and went in like I always done and he was in his chair in the living room. The TV was on. Even as I called out to him I knew. When he didn't turn around or get up, I froze. I mean, my knees went weak and I couldn't move. Eventually I turned and left. I came home and called nine-one-one. I told them I thought something must be wrong since he wouldn't answer his door or his phone. In minutes the sirens filled the street. I felt sick. I can't believe I just left him there.'

There was a crack in Mr. Jeffrey's voice. When I looked at him, he had a palm driven into one of his eyes as if to staunch a wound. He stayed that way for a moment, shook his head once, and gulped his beer. Again, I didn't know what to say. I realized then how close he must have been to my father and I felt something like envy pass through me, though it was so fleeting I could barely sense the feeling let alone name it. What lingered was more like relief. Really, I was thankful my father had had this friendship. In my mind I had always pictured him in his armchair, unmoving, alone, on the verge of tears, her picture in his lap, no contact besides work with the outside world save the flickering noise of the TV or the low sound of the radio, neither of which he took much notice of at all. I was glad for the possibility of some happiness in his life.

I pushed myself from the chair and saw Mr. Jeffrey bent over one of the worktables. He was planing a length of wood, which sounded something like the slick sound of skis in snow.

.   .   .

It was nearly ten when we pulled up to Laura's Tea Room in Mr. Jeffrey's truck.

'We'll grab a couple coffees and go see Jones about the house.' Sitting in the cab he touched my shoulder and looked at me. 'We'll keep the Irish out of these ones though, hey?'

He gave a little laugh and exited the truck. I followed.

Again—with what he said and the off-paternal way he said it—he reminded me of Norman Scott. It occurred to me then that I hadn't seen Norman since just after the episode at the high school. When he came to tell me he didn't believe what was being said about me. I made a promise to myself to drop in on him before heading back to Toronto and my eventual return to Ireland. I thought about asking him to come along, see the literary sites of the Emerald Isle, help me get The Toque & Hoodie off the ground. To be honest, I didn't think I could do it alone.[35]

There were a few locals scattered at different tables inside Laura's Tea Room. Mr. Jeffrey took off his cap and I followed him in. I recognized some of the people and nodded. They looked at me as though they didn't know who I was and maybe they didn't. Mrs. Jeffrey emerged from behind a swinging door on the

---

[35] I realize, in rereading this, that until now I haven't mentioned how I always planned to return to Dun Laoghaire after exacting my revenge on Richards. Teaching was done for me. I knew that. Home was no longer home. Hadn't been in years, really. The plan was to return and open a bar called The Toque & Hoodie, which is where I sit writing this now. I was drinking too much. I knew that too. I figured, maybe if I surrounded myself with the stuff, made it my business so to speak, I wouldn't feel the urge to indulge so much. Twisted logic, I know, but it seems to have worked for the most part. I still have a few now and then but nothing like before. From the outside it appears I've found success. But I have to admit I'm left wondering what good any of it is without you.

other side of the counter at the same time her husband was rais-
ing a hand, issuing a general good morning to the room.

Swaying slightly on his way to the counter, Bill grazed a chair
and the legs scraped the floor. He laughed and spoke to no one
in particular. 'Should watch where I'm stepping.'

I wasn't sure how much my own movement had been com-
promised by the morning's libations, but watching Bill made me
more aware.

Mrs. Jeffrey poured and handed her husband two coffees
without saying a word. He looked at her and smiled, seemingly
unaware of her growing anger.

'Good morning, Mrs. Jeffrey. And how are you this lovely
winter's morning?'

She leaned over the counter and spoke in a firm but quiet
voice, able somehow to retain a contradictorily pleasant look on
her face. An innate skill women seem to have for dealing with the
ceaseless irritation caused by the irreparable idiocy of the men in
their lives.[36]

'Bill Jeffrey. It's ten in the morning.'

. I couldn't see his face but I imagined his eyes opening a little wider. That stunned look of an animal.

'What were you thinking?'

I'm sure she also meant, What were you thinking, bringing
him here?

He shook his head but only slightly. 'I don't know. It's
just—'

'Just nothing. Take the coffee and go home before you
embarrass yourself any further.'

---

[36] I know this only from observation, not from personal experience. There
have been no significant women in my life. None but you. Which may
sound silly, I know, for the amount of time we've spent together. But it's
true. I sometimes imagine us as a middle-aged couple, out in public somewhere, grocery shopping maybe, you getting annoyed by one of my many
idiosyncrasies and having to speak to me the way Mrs. Jeffrey spoke to her
husband that morning I walked into the Tea Room with him drunk before
ten. Strange as it may sound, it makes me smile—the thought of us as that
couple.

Mrs. Jeffrey didn't acknowledge me. The only way I knew she had seen me at all was the second coffee she had given her husband. Thinking back on it, I know she wasn't angry with him for the state he was in (it's not like he was staggering), but far more because I was there. Her anger had everything to do with me.

Bill turned to the room, which made everyone look away. He handed me one of the cups and I followed him out.

My hand on the door, I stopped at the sound of Mrs. Jeffrey's voice. I'm sure she tried to contain herself, but the urge to say something must have been too great. I don't blame her. I had it coming.

'And you should be ashamed of yourself, Benjamin Dunn. Your poor father, rest his soul, was a good man. A good man. He deserved better.'

I didn't turn around but I did pause for a moment so that she knew I'd heard her. It was the least I could do.

.   .   .

We didn't see Jim Jones that morning. As a matter of fact, I didn't see anyone else from Castorville before I left, and if I had to guess now, Bill Jeffery would be the last person I'd ever see from my hometown again.

After leaving Laura's Tea Room we climbed into Bill's truck and sat there for a while looking out the windshield. Once again, I didn't know what to say. Eventually he turned the key over and returned us to Railway Street where we sat in the driveway and stared out the windshield some more. When he finally cut the engine I told him I was sorry. He nodded, not dismissively, and climbed out of the truck. Fighting the catch in my throat, I followed.

In his garage, over one more beer, we made arrangements to sell my father's house. We did what we thought we had to legally. I signed the deed over to Bill and signed a note stating I was entrusting all responsibility to him. I gave him Emerson's phone number and address in Heron River. He was the most responsible, most reliable person in my life, I told Bill. He could send the check there and I'd be sure to get it. If he ever needed to get in touch with me, Emerson would be the man to do it through. I wanted Bill to agree to take a percentage from the sale of the house but he would have none of it. I knew better than to insist.

Once the house business was settled I asked him if he knew where I could pick up a decent vehicle on short notice. I told him I needed it today and could pay cash. Without saying a word he gestured for me to follow him across the snow-covered lawn that spanned the two houses. We crunched through the snow and stomped our feet at the top of the driveway. Looking at me, he reached out and turned the garage door handle, lifted, and revealed the truck sitting inside. The one sitting in Bill's driveway was its twin.

'I convinced him last summer when I bought mine. They took three thousand off the top of each for buying two. Country dealership. Nothing like you'd get in the city.'

I had never known my father to own a vehicle. To my knowledge he'd lived the latter half of his life within a radius of no more than a kilometre.

'Had my old truck for fifteen some-odd years, and when I started talking about a new one I could sense your father was interested himself. I brought an extra brochure home and left it on his kitchen table. Next time I was over I flipped through it and saw where he'd circled different models. I said to him, *So what do you think, Walter*, and you know what he told me?'

I shook my head.

'Pouring the tea he shrugs and says, *Couldn't hurt.*'

Bill laughed and walked into the garage and opened the driver's side door.

'Like I thought. Keys in the ignition.'

He held out an open hand as if he were offering to help someone down from the cab.

'I'm sure he would've wanted you to have it.'

I thought of the last time I saw my father, when he gave me the tin box full of money (which, incidentally, still had enough in it to get me properly started in Ireland), and here I was taking from him again.

Question for Booker: when you take something that's offered is it really taking or is it a kind of acceptance, and if it *is* a kind of acceptance is there a sense of approval that comes with it?

I climbed in. The cab smelled new but there was a trace of him in the air. Like in the house. I'd read somewhere that when someone dies, physical vestiges of him remain in the places he lived. Impossible to see but there nonetheless. It was a detail I took some comfort in.

'Stop by Harrison Ford on your way to the city. They'll take care of the ownership for you.'

I looked at him. I didn't think I'd heard him right.

He nodded. 'I know. You wouldn't believe how many people stop just because of the name. I asked the owner one time if he was really a Harrison. Like he was doing a commercial or something he gives me this line. *Our name is our business.*'

I smiled. 'A name can do a lot.'

'It can.'

He told me to watch myself and he shut the door.

I put both hands on the wheel and stared out the windshield at the door to the house. There was no reason for me to go back in. I started the engine and lowered the window.

'Well, I guess that's it then.'

He touched the side of the truck like it was an animal he was fond of and spoke without looking at me. 'I'll get a fair price for the house.'

I nodded. 'We'll be in touch.'

It was something to say, but even as I said it I knew it wasn't true and so did he.

I slipped the truck into reverse, put my right arm around the headrest of the empty seat, and navigated my exit through the back window. I backed onto the road, and as I was about to pull away Bill came jogging out to the truck, my backpack slung over his shoulder. I'd set it down by the porch the night before when I was looking for the house key. I lowered the passenger window as he approached and he dropped the bag onto the seat. The tin box clunked inside.

'Thanks, Bill.'

I looked at him and tried to make it meaningful. He pressed his lips together and nodded. Then he slapped the side of the truck and held a hand in the air as he moved backwards onto the snow-covered yard where I'd grown up. Where the *For Sale* sign would be driven. Where some other young family, I imagined, might have a better go of it. I watched Bill and the house grow small in the rearview mirror as I drove away, erasing as I went any trace on Railway Street of the family Dunn.

·   ·   ·

The cemetery was just south of town. It was the last thing you saw going and the first thing you saw coming, although it came to be one of those things you didn't really notice at all, especially in winter, unless you had reason, like I did, to stop. I told myself I'd turn in only if there was no sign of anyone else there.

I slowed down so I could scan the few acres of headstones as I passed. At first glance there were no people or vehicles I could see. I looked harder. I wanted a reason not to enter. I'd been in a cemetery only once in my life. For my uncle John's interment. I was ten. All I remember is the ticking of the winch, the lowering of the casket, the minister intoning, 'Ashes to ashes, dust to dust . . .' Being here now, more than fifteen years later, I didn't know what I was supposed to do. I didn't see the purpose in visiting a grave, to be honest. It's not like he was there, waiting for me in his armchair in front of the TV. It's not like he'd hear anything I said. The chance for forgiveness had gone long ago.

I didn't notice the gate drawn across the entrance until I turned in. I felt relief but even more guilt for feeling relief, and just as I began backing up to leave I stomped on the brakes.

Get out and check the gate. He was your father for Christ sake. I mean, really, what kind of son are you? What a piece of work you are.

I sighed, put the truck in park, and climbed down. There was no lock on the latch. I freed the chain from the post and swung the gate open. More like shoved and pulled and inched it open. It took a lot of effort with the snow. So much that I was sweating by the end of it, despite the negative temperature, and breathing heavily. I felt a little less guilty, but not much.

I knew where he'd be buried. Like the whereabouts of the condensed milk the final resting spot of the Dunns inside this country cemetery was information I carried unconsciously within me. The type of knowledge that sits dormant until a situation arrives which requires it. Then it surfaces and you find yourself able to utter it without effort, as obtainable as your own name when someone asks you who you are.

I stood there a moment and oriented myself. When I started to walk I pointed and spoke out loud, as though someone were there with me and had asked where we were headed.

'North-west corner.'

I thought of Booker. I saw his face. Like Oz. Smiling, beaming. He spoke to me in a loud, affected, God-ish voice. He said, 'I am but mad north-north-west. I know a hawk from a handsaw.'

It made me laugh out loud. I looked around and spoke to the trees. 'Just to note, I'm not mad. I'm a little drunk, but I'm not mad.'

I walked towards my father's grave trying to remember the lines that follow 'What a piece of work is a man.' I knew the gist, but I wanted it exactly. There was something about remembering passages verbatim—like hearing a favourite song—which gave me comfort. I think it's because I had to work at it. Unlike Booker, who had to hear or read something only once, I had to focus to recall particular lines. Think deeply. Use contexts. Conjure key images. When all the words finally resurfaced and fell beside one another in the right order, there came with them such pleasure, such calm, that the experience stripped me of all immediate worry and negative thought. Yet it was a feeling, as though in a fairytale, that lasted only as long as the passage itself. Always with the last word came the return of my guilt and anxiety. And I couldn't simply go back to the beginning and repeat the lines again. It didn't work that way. It wasn't like reapplying a balm when the soothing effects wore off. A passage is like a moment. Here and then gone. In the end, everything which is good is good only because it is in the absolute now and because it is fleeting, like the present itself, where the past lingers and the future looms.

It didn't take me long to find the headstone. Behind and around it were markers for other Dunns: my father's paternal grandparents, his own mother and father, his brother who died in a car accident at seventeen, and four sets of uncles and aunts. There had been, at one time, a large family. Now there was none. I remembered the funeral of the last uncle who died. Uncle John. It was the one time I'd been in the cemetery. Besides my father he was the only one in the group I'd known.

The thought of him made me smile and then, finally, I wept. Standing there in the snow, feet burning from the cold, I wept for my father, and it was the first time in my life I'd felt such a permanent loss press down upon me. I ached with it. I didn't know what to do, if there was something I was *supposed* to do, if simply being there was enough. Who would know and what did it matter if they did?

I thought maybe I should say something but I didn't know what. I wiped my eyes, and for some reason I can no longer recall, but which made sense to me at the time, I read the names of all the Dunns I could see out loud, ending with my uncle John. With his name came the words of a poem I knew. Feeling the catch in my throat again, I looked at the headstone in front of me and spoke to my father.

'Since thou and I sigh one another's breath, whoever sighs most is cruellest, and hastes the other's death.'

I never knew him to sigh. Ever.

I wish I could see him. I wish I could shake his hand and tell him how sorry I was. I wish I'd been there. I wish the act of writing had magic enough in it to bring back the dead and undo the wrongs of men. I wish. I wish.

'Jesus H Christ and all the other deities whose names express surprise' —he clapped my shoulders and squeezed, which hurt a little— 'Benjamin Frederick Dunn. Teacher Man of the streets. How the fuck are you, my son?'

Norman Scott, retired Head of English, Heron River High School, stood barefoot in his doorway wearing jeans and a white linen shirt rolled to the elbows, unbuttoned to the sternum. His hair, still without a fleck of grey, was past his ears and wavy, and his Sean Connery beard had gotten away from him. He looked like he'd spent a year in the woods and was just now returning to civilization. He looked like Hemingway, the later years, only a little wilder and fitter.

Without giving me a chance to answer, he slung an arm around my neck and ushered me in, made a show of looking past me into the street.

He leaned in. Spoke in a serious tone. 'Anyone see you?'

I shook my head.

'Good.'

He pulled me by him and shut the door, touched his nose to the glass of the small opaque half-circle window, put a hand by his face and made it look like he was really straining to see out.

'I don't see him. Yet.'

He seemed a little crazy, to be honest. Anyone who knew him could see there was always that possibility. Fashionably crazy, though. Not certifiable. Markedly eccentric. Endearingly quirky.

I looked around. The inside of his house was like a cabin, only polished and organized. High ceilings. Grand, slow-moving fans. Wood. And more wood. Shelves of books everywhere. The whole place smelled of books and wood. Hemingway again, minus the trophy heads on the walls.

'We'll know if he saw you in a minute. He'll thump on that door so hard you'd swear his fist was going to come clean through it.'

I pictured a fist driving a splintered hole through the heavy wooden door.

'If he does come, we'll run you out the back. I'll stall him while you sneak around front and make a run for your truck. I'd hate to see him get his hands on you.'

I had no idea who or what he was talking about.

'I tried telling him you didn't do it. But he's stubborn. It's amazing what people will believe.' He pressed his lips together, shook his head. 'You're a brave soul, coming back here.'

'Jesus, if you're trying to scare me, Norman, you're doing a pretty good job.'

He didn't say anything, only looked at me.

'Well? Are you going to tell me what you're talking about?'

He sighed. 'Remember Big Joe? He lives down the street. He was pretty upset by what you did—sorry, what they *say* you did. He told me, and I quote, *If I ever see that loathsome little lech 'round these here parts again, I'll lynch the lily-livered little leprechaun.*'

When I think back on it, I can see him grin right here. I should've caught on—the alliteration, the cowboy diction, the dramatic earnestness—but I missed it. He had me. Classic Norman.

'Joe?' I furrowed my brow, shook my head. 'Why would Joe care? What's it got to do with him whether I did it or not?'

'Hates anything to do with drugs. Beer and whiskey only. Anything else is immoral. Lowly. Godless.'

'Godless. I didn't peg him for the religious type.'

'He's not. But he's traditional. And rigid in his ways.'

I wiped my brow, felt the heat rise within me. 'Well, listen— I mean—I don't know—if he—'

The fist against the door was sudden and thunderous. The voice that followed, angry and impatient. I don't know how I managed not to piss myself. I must have been a riot to watch. I leapt like a cat and landed with my knees bent, my hands out in front of me like a wrestler.

'Holy fuck. What do I do?'

How Norman didn't break down in hysterics is beyond me.

'Quick. Through the kitchen in the back.'

He pointed and I ran through the house, eyes wide, heart racing. I heard the front door open behind me, voices whispering together, then, 'Where'd he go? I'm gonna kill him.'

I was stuck. Foiled by one of those sliding glass doors with the lever-lock, the vertical bolt penetrating the frame at the top, and the easily missed length of two-by-two sitting in the track at the bottom. It was the two-by-two that got me. I reefed and reefed on that door, but it didn't move. I was caught and I knew it. I've never been any good under pressure.

'Hey.'

I turned, slowly, and saw Big Joe standing there, the width of the kitchen table separating us. Norman was at the fridge, his back to us, doing his best not to laugh no doubt.

I looked at Joe, his eyes full of fury. I didn't know what to say. I was genuinely scared.

He spoke in a low tone. Firm but not loud. Through his teeth. Like an angry parent in public not wanting to draw attention to himself. 'Get over here.'

I moved around the table towards him, head down, eyes averted. Like the child who knows it would be far worse to disobey. 'Listen, Joe, I—'

'Shut up.'

I felt the heat in my face, the catch in my throat. It took everything I had to hold it there.

I heard Norman. 'Take him out back, Joe. I don't want him bleeding in here.'

Bleeding? Jesus. What happened to *I'd hate to see him get his hands on you*? Fucking help me for Christ sake, Norman. Don't give him direction.

I stood there, immobilized and made dumb by my own pathetic surrender. Like a prisoner kneeling for the guillotine. I closed my eyes just as he took me in a headlock. I thought, This is it you sad, sorry lump, and you deserve every bit of what you get.

But instead of the broken nose and the blinding pain I expected, I felt his knuckles raking my scalp. It took me a few seconds to realize he was laughing and not roaring like an animal full of rage. After a few seconds he let me go. Regaining my balance, I stood there rubbing my eyes. The top of my head burned.

Big Joe was pointing at me, holding his own stomach, laughing. Grinning through his beard, Norman handed Joe and me a beer.

My heart settled. I nodded and grinned. 'Fair enough. I deserve worse.'

I felt Joe's big hand slap me on the back. He stopped laughing and wiped his eyes. 'Don't be so hard on yourself. None of us is innocent.'

Norman agreed, and with an actor's voice summed it all up in a single line, sage that he is. 'It takes but a single word to ruin a man, true or otherwise, and a million more to begin the right.'

.   .   .

We sat and drank our first beer and then another, and for some reason I felt more at home there in Norman's kitchen than I had sitting in my father's back on Railway Street. Like Bill Jeffrey, neither Norman nor Joe said anything about my removal from the school. They asked only if I figured the dust had settled, and whether I was back for good. I told them no, I was only back for a day or two, and said I didn't think the dust ever settled after a mess like the one I'd found myself in. They said I was probably right and Norman asked me what I planned to do.

I shrugged. 'Head back to Ireland.'

He nodded. 'I'd heard that's where you went.'

'Yeah, sorry I didn't stop by before I left. It's just—'

'Hey. No apologies. No explanations. You don't need to justify anything to me.' Norman grinned through his beard and leaned forward. 'I am curious though. Was it for a woman?'

'Was what?'

'Ireland.'

I nodded.

He sat back in his chair and drank. 'I thought so. Good for you.'

Norman had never married. A lifelong bachelor and happy about it.

'Is that why you're going back?'

I shook my head. 'Ended badly. I don't think she'd be interested.'[37]

'Ah well, it happens' —he shrugged— 'I wouldn't worry. There'll always be another.'[38]

Joe swallowed a mouthful of beer and shook his head. 'Don't listen to him. You find her whoever she is.'

Joe wasn't married either, as far as I knew. It surprised me, what he said. How serious he was.

'There's nothing better in this world than the love of a good woman.'

He was a little old-fashioned in his diction but I knew what he meant.

Norman winked at me and spoke to Joe. 'Sure there is, Joe— the love of two good women. At the same time.'

We all laughed—the expected reaction—and finished our beer, fulfilling our fixed roles as men.

After a while Norman slapped the table and pushed himself from his chair. 'We need music and more beer.'

He collected the empties and returned them to the case on the counter. I could hear the bottles clanking behind me. Then from the speakers above us, in the four corners of the ceiling, came Gordon Lightfoot singing Early Morning Rain.

Joe leaned in. 'Seriously, though. You find her.'

.   .   .

Norman returned with three more bottles of beer. Lightfoot did The Wreck of the Edmund Fitzgerald, then Stan Rogers took over. I could almost smell the sea.

---

[37] Just so it's clear, you *are* the reason I returned.

[38] No. There won't.

It was coming on five o'clock and I hadn't eaten a thing all day. Ten hours ago I was drinking Irish coffee with Bill Jeffrey, enough that I shouldn't have been driving that truck sitting outside, and now here I was about to snap the cap off another beer. I *was* drinking too much. But what could I do? There are certain times when alcohol is almost mandatory, which won't make any sense to those who don't indulge. But it's true.

So. We drank. And Norman asked me more about Ireland.

'What are you going back for, if not the girl?'

'I like it there. It's not here, you know?'

He nodded. 'What are you going to do, teach?'

I shook my head. 'My teaching days are done.'

Joe banged his beer on the table. 'Me too. Two weeks to go and that's all she wrote for me.'

Norman and I touched the necks of our bottles to Joe's and drank.

'Good for you, Joe.'

'You're fucking right, good for me.'

'So tell us, Joe' —this was Norman— 'what are you going to do in the wake of your glorious teaching career?'

'I'm going to launch that big fucking sailboat sitting in my driveway and see where the wind takes me.'

I raised my bottle. 'To where the wind takes you.'

Joe and Norman raised their bottles to mine and we all drained what was left. Joe let out a big sigh.

'But for now, I say we let the wind blow us down to the Banjo & Axe and get loaded drunk.'

Norman leapt from his chair and mimed what he said. 'Hoist the mainsail! Drop the jib!'

He looked the part. Standing there with his beard and sea-blown hair, his shirt open at the chest, sleeves rolled to the elbows, forearms all sinewy and wind-weathered, leaning back and hauling hand over hand on an invisible rope, squinting against a make-believe gale.

'Watch your heads boys. We're coming about.'

Joe had his head tipped back, singing along with Neil Young and Harvest Moon.

'There's a full moon rising, let's go dancing in the light. We know where the music's playing, let's go out and feel the night.'

Sails set, Norman feigned fatigue and flopped into his chair, squinted into the imaginary moon, and belted out the words with Big Joe and Old Neil. I joined them and we all sang, 'Let's go out and feel the night.'

And so, out we went.

I shouldn't have driven that truck. I should've told them to call a cab. But before I knew it Norman and Joe had climbed in the passenger's side and were waiting for me to usher us into a night of certain debauchery. Again, what was I supposed to do? I could manage an innocuous little five minute ride into town. It was what, Monday? We certainly wouldn't draw any attention on the road. But it wasn't the ride in that worried me. It was the ride out.

Skip ahead a few hours. Marty and Smitty, the other two founding members of the DH, joined us at the Banjo & Axe around eight. Norman, Joe, and I were well on our way. I was at that point where a man thinks he can go on forever. I'd reached the mountaintop. Nothing left for me to grab onto but sky. Followed by the inevitable descent.

Eleven o'clock came and with it the announcement of last call. The chairs were up and we were the only ones left in the place. I hollered at the bartender, showed him two fingers, and drew a circle around my head.

I slapped the table. 'Two more boys. The night ain't over yet.'

Marty let out a big yawn which rippled around the table.

Norman checked his watch. 'I'm fuck'n licked, kid. I gotta go home.'

The others echoed his sentiment.

'Ah, come on. How often do I get to see you guys?'

Almost never. If I thought about it, I'd only ever spent a handful of nights with them in total. I didn't really know them at all.

'We'll do it again, kid. In Ireland'—Norman yawned—'once you're settled and you open that bar of yours.'

It was a nice thing to say.

'Fuck'n right. We'll make it an annual thing.'

'Sure, kid'—he stifled another yawn—'sure.'

They all stood and dug in their pockets for money.

I slapped the table again and they each looked at me. 'Your money's no good here, gentlemen.'

Norman paused and stuck out his hand. He was wavering.

'It's been good seeing you, kid.'

I felt the catch in my throat which is even harder to hold back when you're drunk. My voice cracked a little when I shook his hand and told him how good it had been to see him, too. I shook hands with Marty and Smitty. They thanked me for the pints and I told them there was no need. *There's no need.* It was my pleasure. Joe squeezed my hand so hard it collapsed on itself. He said he hoped he hadn't scared me too much earlier. I tried to regain some sense of grip and told him I knew he was kidding all along. He laughed and clapped me on the shoulder, which hurt a little. He said if I ever needed anything, just call. It was another nice thing to say.

And there I was, alone in a bar, glass in hand, drunk as a loon, wondering where I should go from here. The bartender was cleaning up. I thought about hiding in the washroom until he'd locked the place and left. I could sleep in a booth. The seats were plush and wide enough. All a man in my state needs ever to do is lay his head down somewhere and close his eyes.

The bartender turned the music up and went about mopping the floor. He saw me and said he was locking up in ten minutes. I nodded and asked if he knew of anywhere else that was still open.

'On a Monday night?'

He turned and continued on.

Through the speakers in the ceiling I heard the machine switch CDs. The music started again and it was Johnny Cash playing Sunday Morning Coming Down. I leaned back in the booth and smiled. For the moment I was without guilt and the glass felt fine in my hand. I tapped the table and stretched my legs underneath. I closed my eyes and let the voice wash over me like late night thunder and rain. I heard someone on the radio once say that he was the rare kind of singer who made you stop and listen, no matter who or where you were. I don't know how you measure that kind of claim, but it was true for me.

(*Aside.* Speaking of what is true, there's still no way I can hang my head that doesn't hurt.)

Even as I staggered out of the bar and climbed into the cab of my father's truck I knew the night was going to end badly. I could see what was going to happen like it was scripted. There was no way for me, as the main player, to ignore the words in front of me. The irony is I was the one writing them. It's like I didn't know I had the ability to cross something out or crumple up a page and toss it away if it felt wrong for some reason I couldn't quite explain. I think that's always been my problem: not recognizing my own ability to do something about the situation I was in. Another fault of mine, while we're on the subject, is doing or saying something without taking the time to jump ahead a little, look back at myself, and change what needs to be changed. For the sake of comparison, the Prince had the opposite problem: too much thought. I have to believe there is some kind of amendable middle.[39]

McKnight's was two streets over from the Banjo & Axe, down near the river which was frozen now and covered with snow. Still and scored with the tracks of winter travelers. Snowmobilers, skiers, snow-shoers, ice surfers. Carved paths in snow which appeared to be permanent.

McKnight's was a common destination or rest stop for winter river-goers. In fact, it was a common destination or rest stop for travelers in any season. Over the years it had become a reason to come to town and equally as much a reason to return. Emerson had officially taken over the business and, by all accounts, was doing very well. Certainly the last thing he needed was a drunken Ben Dunn staggering through the doors of his establishment on a Monday night, proclaiming the ineffability of the place. But stagger and proclaim I did.

---

[39] And maybe this is it. Writing all of this down, I mean. Maybe the act of writing itself is the perfect marriage of thought and action.

'Would you look at the polish on this fuck'n joint.'

Thankfully, there was no one there but Emerson, Elizabeth-Anne, and the young woman cleaning the floor.

'What is this, the mopping hour? Everywhere I look there's a bucket of soapy water. This must be one hell of a dirty old town.'

I fell into singing The Pogues' tune, but after that I couldn't remember what happened. I knew it must have been bad. Really bad. The complete opposite of anything good. It was months before Emerson would answer or return any of my calls. Even now he has to pretend I'm someone else and leave the room when I call so Elizabeth-Anne doesn't know who he's talking to. Eventually he forgave me for what I did—he is by far the better man—but I know he'll never forget. How could he? That I now know what I did but cannot remember doing it makes it even worse. Part of my pagan penitence I suppose. I'm certain there must be a moment every time he hears my voice—although he assures me he's past the whole ordeal—when he cringes and asks himself why he bothers to remain a friend to such a wretch like me. But remain he does and more thankful I could not be.

Because I wanted to include his account verbatim—to make sure I got the whole thing right—I recorded with his permission the conversation we had in which he retold, at my request, the scene of my incursion. What follows—again, with his express permission—is the transcript of that conversation.

BD: So. Just for record's sake, you know that I'm recording this and plan to include it, word-for-word, in the project I'm working on.

EM: Yes.

BD: I appreciate your candour.

EM: It's not exactly a favour, you realize.

BD: I know. But still, I'm in your debt.

EM: I'm not sure how comfortable I am telling you everything.

BD: Please. Don't leave anything out.

EM: This is it, though. You have to promise never to ask me about it again.

BD: I promise.

EM: I don't know. I don't think I can do it. Some of it, yes. But not all of it.

BD: Pretend it isn't me.

EM: But it is you, Ben. Christ, do I know there's no changing that.

BD: Bless you.

EM: Pardon?

BD: You blasphemed. I figured that must be a little like sneezing for believers. So, bless you.

EM: Funny. You're a funny man, Ben Dunn. You know, finding God wouldn't hurt you any.

BD: I wouldn't know where to look.

EM: Anyway—if I'm going to do this you can't interrupt me.

BD: I won't say a thing.

EM: Not a word.

BD: I promise.

EM: Fine. Here goes then.

(*He clears his throat and waits a full six seconds. Nothing but dead air.*)

I hadn't seen you since the summer. The night of our reunion gig. After the last set I told you I had to get home to Elizabeth-Anne. I said she didn't like being alone in the house at night. I lied. She was at her parents' place. The thing is, I live in this town. This is my home. I run a business here. I have a reputation to uphold. I couldn't be seen staggering around the streets at three in the morning. Besides, I was past all that.

BD: (*Left Shoulder*): Oh, okay, Mr. Morally Fucking Superior.
    (*Right Shoulder*): Shut up, Dunn.

EM: What's more, I didn't like the way things ended with Wyatt. I was upset with you. Don't get me wrong, I think the lifestyle he's chosen is wrong, too. I mean, it says right there in the Bible multiple times—Corinthians, Romans, Exodus, Leviticus—that no man shall lie with another man, but it also warns us not to turn a blind eye, especially on those we love.

BD: Jesus fucking Christ, McKnight. Are you serious?

(*Dead air.*)

BD: McKnight?

EM: (*Quietly.*) Once more, Ben, and I hang up.

BD: Sorry.

EM: I mean it.

BD: I know. I'm sorry. Please, continue.

EM: Anyway, the point was I hadn't seen you in a long time. And then in you walk, unannounced, on some random Monday night in December just as we were about to close, beyond drunk, reckless, a hazard to yourself and everything and every-one in your path. For a long time afterwards, Elizabeth-Anne tried to get me to call the police. She wanted you locked up. I told her I couldn't do that to you. She said, 'Why not? Look what he's done to you.'

(*A pause, a sigh.*)

Maybe I should have.

BD: (*Left Shoulder*): Yeah, maybe you fucking should have, you prick.

(*Right Shoulder*): Listen, you asked for this, and what's more, you had it coming. So shut up.

EM: Anyway, so in you walk, shouting something like, 'Would you look at the bleep-bleep shine on this place,' and you knock over a vase which knocks over another and then another and they smash all over the floor and you look up, hand to your mouth, laughing, and you say, 'Whoops. I hope they weren't too expen-sive.' Not an ounce of remorse in you. They were two-hundred-dollar vases, Ben, and you smashed them. And then laughed about it. Who does that?

BD: (*Left Shoulder*): Who does that? Who pays more than a thou-sand fucking dollars for six vases and then sets them up like domi-noes to be knocked down in the first place?

(*Right Shoulder*): That's not the point. Now for the last time. Shut. Up.

EM: Then, without even being asked, Kendra—you remember Kendra, don't you, Ben? She was a student of yours—

BD: (*Left Shoulder*): Do I sense a touch of sarcasm there, Mr. McKnight? I can play that game, too.

(*Right Shoulder*): Don't you dare.

EM: She set upon the mess you made in such a hurry you'd think she was trying to erase the fact it had even happened. She recognized you as soon as you stumbled through the doors and instantly felt sorry for you. Even after you were gone. Even after the horrible things you said to her. She told me she had always thought you were innocent of what they said you did, that you'd simply run into a pile of bad luck. I used to think so too, but now I'm not so sure. Part of me thinks you take aim at such piles and run headlong into them. Anyway, she said you used to annoy her with your tangents and your obsession with Hamlet and your insistence that there were no right answers, only well-argued ones, but really, when she thought about it—despite your awful display in the restaurant that night, because that wasn't really you, she said—you had been the best English teacher she'd ever had. She even used the word 'favourite,' Ben. How does that make you feel?

BD: (*Left Shoulder*): Am I supposed to answer that?
     (*Right Shoulder*): Don't answer anything, stupid. Just listen.

EM: Well?

BD: I thought you didn't want me to say anything.

EM: I'm asking you a question, Ben. Answering a question is not interrupting. It's called being socially adept.

BD: (*Left Shoulder*): Is that so.
     (*Right Shoulder*): It is. Now answer his question.
     (*Left Shoulder*): You're the one who told me not to.
     (*Right Shoulder*): Well, now I'm telling you *to*.
     (*Left Shoulder*): I don't think I like you.
     (*Right Shoulder*): I'm crushed. Now answer him.
     (*Left Shoulder*): Fine.

   Fine.

EM: What was that?

BD: Nothing. Sorry.

EM: Well?

BD: It makes me feel good, I suppose.

EM: Now see, that's part of the problem, Ben. You feel good when you're supposed to feel bad, and you feel bad when you're supposed to feel good.

BD: (*Left Shoulder*): I don't know what the fuck he's talking about. (*Right Shoulder*): Just say, 'You're right,' and let him continue.

 You're right, Emerson.

EM: (*A sigh.*) Maybe there's hope for you yet, Ben.

BD: Maybe.

EM: You're sure you want me to continue?

BD: Please.

EM: Okay. So, after the vase massacre, you staggered your way behind the bar and proceeded to drink right from the tap.

BD: (*Left Shoulder*): (*Laughs.*) I wish I could remember that.

EM: You looked like Homer Simpson. But not in an endearing, funny sort of way. It was pathetic. Sad. You were a sad, pathetic, real life version of a cartoon, Ben. It was awful to watch. When you finally came up for air, beer was dripping from your chin. The front of your shirt was soaked. Your eyes were closed and there was this monstrous, distorted sort of grin on your face like you'd just crawled up through the cold, thick darkness of the underworld and finally broke through the surface to feel the warm light of freedom on your face.

BD: (*Left Shoulder*): Been working on that one, Father McKnight?

EM: Elizabeth-Anne and I were flabbergasted.

BD: (*Left Shoulder*): Flabbergasted. Oh. Well.

EM: I mean, we couldn't believe what we were seeing, Ben. You went from the tap to the Scotch and started another smashing fit. You took a bottle of Lagavulin, uncorked it, took a swig, and then in some awful country accent, furrowed your brow at us and said, 'Deserve's got nothing to do with it.' Then you smashed the bottle over the counter and it went off like a bomb. You did the same thing with four more bottles, like you were doing multiple takes on the set of some movie.

BD: (*Left Shoulder*): (*Says nothing.*)
      (*Right Shoulder*): Getting bad, isn't it.
      (*Left Shoulder*): (*Says nothing again.*)

EM: Seething, Elizabeth-Anne turned and looked at me, as though I'd invited you or something, as though I were responsible somehow for your behaviour. I had to do something. You were destroying the place.

BD: (*Right Shoulder*): Not so cocky anymore, are we?
      (*Left Shoulder*): Leave me alone.
      (*Right Shoulder*): I'll leave you alone, but it's not me you have to worry about.

EM: So I went behind the bar, hands out in front of me to show I was coming in peace. I moved slowly, cautiously, like I was approaching a strange animal. I thought you'd see me coming, realize what you were doing, and stop. But you didn't. When I was within arm's reach I said your name. Calmly, without an

ounce of anger in my voice, I said, 'Ben—Ben—what are you
doing? It's me, Emerson.' You turned, as though to answer me. I
was trying to smile. At first, so were you. I thought it was over. I
breathed out, said, 'Okay, Ben. It's okay. Let's go. I'll take you
home.' But then, like the word 'home' was some kind of trigger,
your smile morphed into an evil, villainous grin and you started
breathing loudly. Your face went red. Your neck tensed. I saw hate
in your eyes. I started backing up, out around the bar and into the
open. You followed me, chest heaving, face full of rage. I put my
hands out in front me, shook my head, said, 'No, Ben. No. Stop.
It's me, Emerson.' But it was no use. You weren't you. Next thing
I knew I was laid out on the floor. You stood over me, fist drawn
back like the hammer on a gun, like a killer about to finish the
job. I heard Elizabeth-Anne scream as you drove your fist into my
face for a second time. The first blow blackened and swelled my
eye shut. The second broke my nose. For some reason I got up
quickly. Certainly not because I wanted to fight. The hand of
God, maybe, helping me up so I wouldn't drown in my own
blood. My face was a mess. The swelling came quickly around my
eye and blood ran from my twisted nose down my chin, dripping
onto the floor, down the front of my white shirt. I looked like a
monster. Elizabeth-Anne wouldn't stop screaming. You turned to
her, hands in your pockets, calm all of a sudden, and said, 'I bet
that's the most he's ever made you scream.' Her screaming turned
to words. She yelled at you to get out. Over and over. 'Get out!
Get out!' She was about to lunge at you when Kendra, who'd
been witness to the whole incident, grabbed her by both arms
and held her, thank God. She was hysterical. Then, apparently just
noticing her, you looked at Kendra and said, 'Hey, there, little lady.
What about you?' Her eyes were full of disbelief. Even after all
this she still defended you. I can't imagine why. You said, 'You
know, you look familiar. Yeah, I definitely know you from somewhere. Mmn-mmn. Jesus, do I like that red hair. I bet you're one
fiery little number in the sack.' You were nodding. She was shaking her head. Elizabeth-Anne had gone quiet. She was tiring,
breathing heavily. She couldn't do it anymore. She looked defeated. Her eyes closed, she managed to say, 'You son of a bitch, I hope

you burn in hell.' You ignored her. I was trying to stop my nose from bleeding. I held my head back. As calmly as when I approached you behind the bar, I said, 'Ben, you have to leave.' You ignored me, too, folded your arms, and continued to look at Kendra. Forgive me, Father, for repeating what I'm about to repeat, but I think it's important for him to hear it exactly as he said it—

BD: (*Left Shoulder*): Jesus.
       (*Right Shoulder*): Hah. He's sure as hell not going to help you.

EM: This is exactly what you said, Ben. I couldn't believe what I was hearing. I was dumbfounded. When you were done I finally grabbed you by the arm and hauled you out. Luckily, you let me. I think you were beginning to snap out of it. Like you'd just woken from a nightmare. You looked at me. Full of remorse, finally, I could tell. You stuck out a hand for me to shake. You told me you were sorry. Sorry for everything. You looked past me and saw Elizabeth-Anne holding Kendra. They were both crying. You looked at me again and asked me to tell them how sorry you were. I said nothing. I continued to point out the door. Finally, you took back your hand, dropped your head, and left. I don't know what happened to you after that. Part of me worried about where you'd go, but to tell the truth, I didn't lose any sleep over it. I was relieved. I never wanted to see you again. In the moment, I hated you, Ben. I've never hated anyone before. But I hated you.

       Okay, so here it is. This is what you said, Ben. As though the rest of what you did weren't bad enough. Prepare yourself, because you'll never forget it once I tell you. It'll haunt you, like it's haunted me. Only worse. But you need to know. It's part of your atonement. I agree with you now. I need to tell you. Now that I've come this far. Now that I've told you this much. You need to know it all.

       So here it is. Word for awful word. This is what you said. To Kendra. An eighteen-year-old former student. You looked at her—and God, I ask you again to please forgive me for repeating this—you looked at her and said, 'Mm-mm-mmn. God damn do I like the look of you. Fuck me, but you're making me hard. Just look at you. Mm-mmn. Perky little titties. Hard little body. But fuck. Tightest of tight little pussies, I bet. I'm starting to quiver just thinking about it. Mm-mmn. You know, little lady, I got me a comfy little truck out there I just inherited from my old man. He up and died at fifty-three. You believe that? No sign of anything the matter with him. Oh, well. Whatever. He was a pussy. Probably what killed him, being a pussy. I'm not a pussy. You can bet on that. I swore I'd never be a pussy. One thing I never wanted to be was a pussy. Pussy, pussy, pussy. Fuck but I bet you have a nice one though. Tight and warm. Red, I bet. Shaved maybe. Mm-hmn. Fuck would I love to get a lick. What do you say there, little fire? You and me go get properly acquainted in that truck I stole from my dead, good-for-nothing, pussy of an old man. I'll lick your little lolly till you shake. Let's blow this pop-stand and go fuck till we can't fuck no more.'

BD: (*Left Shoulder*): Jesus.

(*Right Shoulder*): Like I said. He's not going to help the likes of you.

EM: Ben?

BD: (*Says nothing.*)

EM: That's it, Ben. That's all of it.

BD: (*Says nothing again.*)

EM: Ben? Say something so I know you're there. So I know you heard me. So I know I didn't just say all of that for nothing.

BD: I wish I'd never asked.

EM: There's no point in wishing, Ben.

BD: I know. I know that too well.

EM: (*Sighs.*) I feel better. I didn't think I would. But I do.

BD: That's good. I've never felt worse.

EM: Then there's still hope for you.

BD: McKnight?

EM: Yes, Ben.

BD: I hate to crush your endearingly optimistic outlook on life—but hope's a cock tease. Hope's a crock of shit. Hope is the tiny little light bouncing on the horizon of the sea for the lost and abandoned man struggling in the waves of the cold, dark, infinite water—hanging onto life only because of the pathetic possibility which the light torturously inspires, however miniscule and ridiculous that possibility is. Hope is the only reason God exists at all. For the flock of the lost and the abandoned bobbing like driftwood in the sea of his creation, naïve enough to believe that that tiny little distant light is there for them. To show them the way. To lead them to paradise. But if they looked hard enough—if they took the time to step back and really look—they would see that there is no light. They would see that it's a phantom, put there by the weak part of the brain. The hopeful part. The desperate part. Far, far off in the distance. So far off—yet close enough still to see—that it's impossible, ultimately, to fully prove or disprove its existence. Regardless, proof or no proof, God's a cock tease. So fuck him, McKnight. Fuck him and his doctrine of hope. I have no hope. I don't have a hope in hell.[40]

.   .   .

---

[40] I was in a state. I don't really believe all of that. How could I? Hope is all I have left of you.

I still don't remember anything about that night past the point of walking into my friend's restaurant and singing Dirty Old Town. But I know about it now. And knowing is far worse than remembering.

When I woke up I was in the back seat of the truck, parked at the end of the pier in Rafter's Park. If the good people who designed the pier hadn't included a concrete enclosure at the head of it, I'm certain I'd have driven right off the edge, gone through the ice, and slowly sank, the dark, lightless water pouring into the cab around me.

There wasn't room to turn around on the pier so I had to back up the length of it. I kept the tires in the tracks I'd made in the snow on the way out. It was ten in the morning. If it had been the summer, the pier would've have been lined with people. As it was, there wasn't a soul. In the distance I could hear the violent whine of snowmobiles. I imagined myself on one, heading straight for the concrete enclosure. Eyes wide and dancing, raised the instant before contact, screaming, 'Hallelujah! Hallelujah!' If nothing else, it would have been a dramatic end.

My head pounded and my insides felt ripped apart. The coffee I bought on the way out of town made it worse. I stopped four times on the way to the city to throw up on the side of the road. Each time felt like an exorcism. But the demons remained. Locked up and heavy with chains within me. Although I couldn't remember what I'd done the night before, I knew I'd done something awful. The guilt was thick. Blood thick.

Dunn, I told myself, you deserve the hell you're in.

I saw a flash of myself behind the bar. Bottle raised above my head. Evil in my eyes. Snarling the rebuttal, 'Deserve's got nothing to do with it.'

.   .   .

I made it into the city, bought a handheld video camera, and locked myself in a hotel room for three days. I went sober. I needed things to change. I needed something to go right. I focussed on Richards and the plan. I contacted Vicky Fern. She told me

Richards had taken the bait. He was excited and honoured to win the award and looked forward to the interview. He hardly ever got into the city these days. She mimicked his diction and general pretentiousness, which made me laugh but also stirred the anger within me and made me even hungrier for revenge.

She was set to meet him at Bon Hommes Friday evening at seven. She would sit in the same booth we had sat in when I met her there a few days ago. I would be there at quarter to, unrecognizable, I hoped, in my ball cap and shades, tucked away in a nearby booth with a good line of sight.

I practiced using the camera and rehearsed what I was going to say to him after I'd caught him on film with Vicky's 'friend,' who I hoped was as good an actor as she was. The whole plan depended on how believable his interlude with Richards was.

Here's what I intended to tell Richards. I'd been thinking about it a lot, rehearsing it in the mirror. I'd look him in the eye and tell him if he didn't do exactly what I asked—if he didn't march into Eckleburg's office on Monday morning and tell her he had made the video of me allegedly selling drugs to a student solely out of spite and wanted nothing more than to see me ruined, if he didn't tell her that I was a good and honest man and deserved nothing less than a retraction of all allegations and convictions sent down by the school and the Board, if he didn't insist on my license being reinstated, if he didn't ask for me to be apologized to both privately and publicly, and, if I wanted it, offered my old job back—if he didn't do and say all these things, I would upload the amorous file of him and the man stroking him off in a booth at Bon Hommes, title it *Richards' Reunion w/ Former Student*, and send it to every staff member at the school and copy every teacher on the Board. I would upload it to YouTube. In a week there would be a million views. It would ruin him, like he ruined me.

Friday. Vengeance day. Checkout was at noon. I'd been sober for three full days and I was feeling great. I hadn't felt this driven and directed since undergrad and the days of The River's Edge. I was convinced the plan Booker and I had devised would work. Richards would have no choice but to submit to my demands. My name would be cleared and I would accept all apologies with grace and humility. I would respectfully decline the offer to return to teaching and buy a one-way ticket to Ireland. I would open The Toque & Hoodie, find Aislinn, apologize, and begin my new life. I couldn't have felt better.

So I went to a pub for lunch and had three pints. Just enough to loosen up the muscles of the brain and feel a little warmth. I told myself I deserved it.

I spent the afternoon walking around downtown. Another glorious winter's day. I stopped by two more pubs, nursed a beer in each, and before long the sun went down and it was past six. Less than an hour to show time. I made my way to Bon Hommes, tucked myself in a booth out of the way, and waited.

Gregory J saw me come in. He brought me a pint and wished me luck. Vicky must have told him about our little play, which was probably the smart thing to do. It was ten minutes to the hour. I was hyper-aware. My knee was bouncing beneath the table and my eyes were wide and unblinking behind the sunglasses I wore. From where I was I couldn't see the door, but I could hear Gregory J greeting someone.

'Oh, yes, of course. I had heard you were coming. What an honour it is to meet you. Ms. Fern will be here soon, I'm sure.'

Duncan, you idiot. Patricia Duncan.

'Sorry, whom did you say?'

It was him alright. I'd have known his voice anywhere. The piss-ant.

'Sorry?'

'You said a Ms. Fern will be here soon. I do believe I am meant to meet a Ms. Duncan. From The Globe & Mail.'

'Oh, yes, of course, Ms. Duncan—' Gregory J sounded flustered. He was going to fuck it all up before it even started. 'You'll have to excuse me. I get the two confused all the time. Ms. Fern's a reporter with the Star. The two are friends and meet here frequently. You can see how I'd mix them up, two lovely Lois Lanes that they are.'

Not bad, Gregory J, not bad. Now just take him to the table and bring him a drink.

'I would not know. I never read the Star.'

I couldn't stand him. It took everything I had not to march over there and drive him right in the face. Screw the plan. Screw the revenge. It would feel so good to drop him with one knuckle-shot to the nose—crunch!—followed by a few kicks to the midsection for good measure.

I was feeling violent. I had to contain myself when he came into view. Gregory J took off Richards' jacket one arm at a time, then his scarf, then Richards handed Gregory J his hat and gloves. Gregory J seated him and showed him the wine list.

After a cursory glance at the list, he sighed, like nothing was quite good enough. 'The house red will have to do.'

'Always a good choice, sir. We serve an excellent Pinot Noir.'

'Excellent.'

'Excellent.'

Gregory J left and returned with a glass and a bottle of red. He poured half an inch, let Richards swirl and sniff it, then filled the glass after Richards gave him the nod of approval.

'Enjoy. I'll escort Ms. Duncan to your table the moment she arrives.'

Richards nodded. Gregory J bowed slightly and took three steps backwards before turning away. He walked past my booth and gave me a wink and a grin. I wanted to stop him and tell him to ease up on the boot-kissing but I didn't want to blow my cover. I gave him a little nod which he appreciated.

It was close to ten minutes past the hour when Vicky arrived. Striding past me without a glance, face a little flushed, she took her coat and accessories off before she arrived at the table. Without pause, she handed everything but her bag to Gregory J, who met her at the table, and extended a hand to Richards who, removing his glasses, looked up and set his book on the table.

'I'm so terribly sorry, Mr. Richards. I do hope you'll forgive me.'

'Oh, not at all. I was engrossed in my book, enjoying my wine. Please' —he gestured across the table— 'have a seat.'

I was in perfect position. The place was still quiet at this hour and I could hear everything they said.

Vicky sat and looked up at Gregory J who had taken her things and returned. 'Chardonnay, please, Mr. J.'

'Of course, Ms. Duncan—and yourself, Mr. Richards? Another glass of the house?'

Richards swirled the remaining mouthful and drained it. 'Why not? It is a celebration.'

Vicky laughed an appreciative sort of laugh and touched Richards' arm. She was good. 'It is a celebration, Mr. Richards. It most definitely is.'

She took a tape recorder, a pad of paper, and a pen from her bag.

'Would it be okay if I recorded some of the interview, Mr. Richards, for the sake of quotational accuracy?'

He put his elbows on the table and folded his hands together, like a pedestal, and set his chin on top. 'Quotational. An interesting word.'

Vicky touched her mouth. 'Oh no, I've flubbed already. Please forgive me. I'm a little nervous. I was so worried I'd misspeak in front of you and there I've gone and done it already. I'm so sorry.'

'Don't be. Language is a mutable organism.'

I could feel the bone of his face on the fist I was making beneath the table. I hated him.

Vicky took the pen and scribbled. She spoke as she wrote. 'Mutable organism' —she set the pen down and looked at him— 'that's wonderful. What a wonderful phrase.'

She was perfect.

'See, any time you are worried that you have made some kind of verbal blunder, or if someone calls you on the correctness of a word, all you need to do is look at him, or her of course, and say, *No need to worry, I am a licensed neologist.*'

He grinned like an idiot.

She took the pen up again and nodded as she wrote. 'What is that, exactly? A neologist.'

Like she had to ask.

'A maker of new words.'

I had a new word for him: burningtobeatyourbastardassdown.

Vicky nodded. 'I'll remember that.'

Gregory J brought their drinks. Richards made a toast. 'To neology and the mutability of our beautiful language.'

I got up from my table, maybe too quickly, and headed for the bathroom. If I was going to be sick I didn't want to puke right there and blow my cover. On my way back I stopped at the bar and asked Gregory J to bring me another pint and a double JD. I needed the blood to settle. I felt like I was going to kill him.

I took a copy of The Globe & Mail from the bar, removed my shades, drew the peak of my cap down low, and hid behind the Lifestyle section. Gregory J brought my drinks and I offed the JD in a gulp. The heat was instant. I felt calmed. I was okay. I'd make it. I had to.

'You know, come to think of it, I'd like to record the whole interview, if that's okay with you, Mr. Richards.'

'Certainly. However you want to do it.'

'It would be great to make it available as a podcast.'

'Absolutely. Yes. A podcast.'

He had no idea what a podcast was.

Peering over the top of the paper, I saw Vicky raise the tape recorder. 'Mr. Richards, I do have to say, it is a privilege to meet such an accomplished teacher. It is plain to see from what the jurors have written—praise in the highest degree—just how extraordinary an educator you really are . . .'

She continued, nearly verbatim, with the speech she'd improvised the day we met.

'That was quite an introduction, Ms. Duncan. Thank you.'

'No, thank you, Mr. Richards. For being so generous with your time. Now, if you'll only bear with me, I have so many questions I want to get to. First, I know the readers of this article will want to know what brought you to teaching. Was it a calling? I mean did you always know you wanted to help develop the minds and shape the collective character of our nation's youth? What is it that motivates you to roll up your sleeves and dig into your work every day? What gives you satisfaction? What makes you tick? What does it mean to be Grant Richards?'

'Well, where do I start? I can remember as a young child always loving school. I learned to read at a young age—two or three, I think—and once they were old enough to sit and listen, I was forever reading to my two younger siblings. I loved having an audience.'

'So you consider teaching a sort of performance?'

'Yes. I suppose I do.'

'Interesting.'

'Anyway, when I was about ten years old I encountered a truly great teacher. Mr. Hennessey. If I had to name a single inspiration, he would be the one. I like to think I approach the profession as he did.'

'And how is that?'

'Selflessly. Openmindedly. Courageously.'

What an arrogant, self-aggrandizing fuck.

'What is it about teaching that requires courage?'

'A better question, Ms. Duncan, would be what doesn't?'

I wanted to walk over there and with as much stunned bewilderment I could muster, place my hands on his table, look him straight in his piss-ant little eyes, and ask, *Did I just hear you use a contraction, Mr. Richards?*

'Everything about teaching requires courage. Walking through the doors of the school every day. Standing in front of a class. Delivering curriculum. Grading papers. Mediating personalities. Motivating the unmotivated. Sitting down with parents. The whole gamut.'

'So what motivates you? Where's the satisfaction?'

Richards took a slow sip of wine, looked at the ceiling as though checking for leaks, and tilted his head like a dog trying to determine the origin of a foreign noise. When he finally answered the question, he gazed off in the distance. He was a parody of himself.

'The students.'

What a crock of shit. My arm was shaking I was squeezing my fist so tight. Vicky tilted her head, touched his arm again.

'That's beautiful, Mr. Richards. You really are one of the good ones. If only there were more like you.'

'Thank you, Ms. Duncan. I should say, though, I do it not to be good but because I know no other way to be.'

My Christ, if I'd had a bat or a crowbar I'd have taken his head clean off.

'Humility is the first sign of greatness, Mr. Richards.'

'How very sagacious of you, Ms. Duncan.'

I was beginning to think the son of a bitch had actually won the award and Vicky really was a young reporter from The Globe & Mail being swept away by her subject.

'And please, call me Grant.'

Grant? He never wanted anyone to call him Grant. (*My name, Mr. Dunn, is not Terry. It is Grant, which you know very well. And I prefer Mr. Richards, as I have told you before, particularly in the professional setting in which we are in. I do believe I have earned it.*)

Earn's got nothing to do with it. Grant.

He reached out and touched Vicky's hand—the one touching his arm—and she let him. She was beyond good. Oscar worthy.

'Okay. Grant.'

'That is better—Patricia is it?'

'It is.'

'Patricia. What a lovely name. Like a flower.'

If he broke into a poem, I was abandoning ship. Screw the plan and the reclamation of my name. I'd walk casually over to their table, punch him in the face a few times, draw a little blood, break his nose maybe, and walk out. I bet that's what Johnny Cash would've done. Clint Eastwood for sure.

'Speaking of flowers, I read somewhere that in addition to the plaque, they present you with a single rose when you go up to accept your award. I was wondering if you might know why that is.'

Masterful, Vicky. Masterful.

Richards clasped his hands and grinned. 'Certainly it must have to do with the symbolism attached to the rose itself. The beauty, the singularity, the dichotomous and simultaneous power and fragility. Come to think of it, I do believe it was Trudeau who began that tradition.'

What a bullshitter. Hemingway would've made a pulpy mess of his face. Trudeau, after stunning him with a bit of French or a quote from Herodotus, would've fed him his fist too I bet.

'You're so knowledgeable, Mr. Rich—I mean, Grant.'

He smiled. 'I read a lot.'

I remembered the bookshelves in Vicky's apartment. Stacked and spilling over. When I asked her, she told me she got through three or four books a week. Though she hadn't meant to impress me, she did.

'How much is a lot?'

'At least a book a week. Sometimes two.'

Vicky grinned. 'That is a lot.'

'I think it is important. People who spend little to no time reading are sorely lacking in much of what it means to be human.'

'I couldn't agree more.'

'Do you read much, Patricia?'

'A little, yes.'

'Have you ever read Richler?'

'I have.'

'And what did you think?'

'He's funny.'

'Really. Hmn.'

'That surprises you?'

'Well, you will forgive me, I hope, but you are a woman.'

I thought I saw her furrow her brow which made me nervous.

'Yes, Mr. Richards. I am.'

'Oh, please, take no offence. I meant only that women usually get upset with Richler. They think he is a misogynist.'

'I don't think so.'

'Believe me. I have read articles.'

'I meant that *I* don't think he is.'

'Oh. Well, how very openminded of you. I do have to say though, I consider myself a feminist and I think he is.'

'But he writes fiction. *He* is not his characters.'

Richards nodded, grinned. 'Yes, but the author's life is really all we have to go on in terms of understanding the work.'

'What about the work?'

'Oh, that is only part of it, Patricia. If you will permit me an analogy, it is like having a lock without the key.'

Vicky finished her wine. Richards followed suit and snapped his fingers above his head.

'Another. Only this time let us make it a Macallan's. In honour of Richler.'

'I'll pass. Scotch never agrees with me.'

'But you are such a congenial young lady.'

He smiled, and he was still smiling when Gregory J arrived.

'That was enough wine for me, my boy. Bring me a Macallan's. Neat. And make it a triple. I am on top of the world tonight.'

'Excellent. And for you, Ms. Duncan?'

She tapped her wine glass.

'Excellent.'

'Yes. Excellent. I am excellent. She is excellent. You are excellent. Macallan's is excellent. The evening is excellent. Excellent, excellent, excellent.'

Gregory J smiled. 'I'm glad to see you're enjoying yourself, Mr. Richards.'

'And why should I not be, young man? I am in the big city being interviewed by a lovely young woman from the country's most respectable newspaper because I have won the Governor General's Award for Teaching. Can you imagine?'

'It sounds like quite an honour, sir.'

'It does. Indeed it does. It does indeed, does it not?'

He laughed. And Vicky and Gregory J laughed with him.

.   .   .

The next hour went by in a similar fashion. Richards was into his second triple. Vicky was still nursing her second glass of wine. I was drilling a hole in the underside of the table with my knee.

Bon Hommes was beginning to fill up with the night crowd. I scanned the faces for Vicky's friend. I'd never met him so there was no way I'd know him, but I looked anyway. He'd recognize me by my position, no doubt, and wink. Then I'd know.

I thought, What if someone winks and it's not him?

Gregory J stopped by. 'Another pint?'

I shook my head. 'Where's this friend of Vicky's.'

'He's here. He's been here about ten minutes.'

'Well, Jesus. What's he waiting for?'

'Vicky's going to excuse herself from the table. That's his cue. He'll move in when she gets up to leave.'

'She told you everything, I suppose.'

'She told me enough.'

'You must think I'm a real asshole.'

'I'm not here to judge. I'm here to serve.'

'How noble of you. But, really, what do you think about what I'm doing?'

'You don't really care what I think, do you Benjamin?'

I did, sort of.

'No. I guess not.'

'You're sure you're alright?'

I was sure I wasn't.

'One more. I'll have one more.'

He left and returned with another pint. I drank a third of it straight off.

There were a lot of people now—almost exclusively men—mingling in the aisle between our two tables. The place was packed. It was going to be difficult to keep a clear line of sight. I'd have to work the zoom. Good thing I'd practiced.

The camera was in the seat beside me. I turned it on, pressed record, hit stop and shut it off. I'd done the same thing about a dozen times since I arrived.

I couldn't hear what Richards and Vicky were saying anymore. I couldn't imagine what she'd still be talking to him about. I trusted her though. I had a good feeling. Right from the first time I sat down with her a week ago in this very place.

I felt a hand on my shoulder. I looked up. It was Vicky, leaning in as she passed by, whispering, 'Show time.'

My heart thumped a little faster. This was it. I fumbled for the camera and dropped it under the table.

'Shit. Fuck.'

I looked around. No one had heard me. It was far too busy. I reached under the table but couldn't put my hand on the camera. I got down on my knees and patted around until I found it.

Worried I'd broken the thing, I turned the camera on, pressed record, hit stop, and shut it off. I sighed. It was alright. The plan was still intact. I went to stand and cranked my head off the table.

'Shit. Fuck.' Louder this time, but when I scrambled to my seat I still hadn't attracted any attention.

I was breathing heavily. I took a few gulps of beer, wiped my brow, and settled. When I checked, Richards was still alone. I set the camera on the table and pointed it towards him, adjusted the zoom. The tiny screen allowed me to set the shot without looking through the viewfinder. I was clandestine in my set-up. Furtive. A real pro.

And then there he was. Vicky's friend. The man of the hour. When it was all said and done, I would raise a glass to this man and pay him double for his fine thespian work.

He was good-looking but not too good-looking. Tall but not tilt-your-head-back-to-look-at-him tall. Fit but not intimidatingly so. Not too young but not too old. In short, like Vicky, he was perfect.

He stopped within the frame and gestured toward the empty seat. Richards nodded and Vicky's friend sat down. Here we go, I thought. Here we fucking go. Revenge, Richards. How sweet it is.

For about a minute all they did was talk. Heads nodding, mouths moving. Like extras in the background, instructed by the director to appear to be in conversation but nothing too animated, nothing too distracting. Forgettable.

I wished I could hear what they were saying. I thought maybe afterwards I could figure out how to filter out all the background noise or dub in some incriminating dialogue. I knew it didn't matter though. I needed action. I needed our leading man to take charge and plant a great big wet one on an unsuspecting Richards, throw a leg over the saddle of his lap and ride him like a bull for a good six seconds before being thrown. That's what I needed. Richards could lose his mind afterwards. Scream. Yell. Hit the guy. It wouldn't matter. I could do a lot with six seconds of footage. I had a few scene-setting shots from earlier and with a bit of editing I could make it look like this was a regular hangout for Richards. I could make it look like he was the one who had called our leading man over to his table and initiated the physical contact. I could make it look like Richards was hammered out of his mind and made a habit of ripping it up in the city. A weekend predator on the prowl for casual encounters. All I had to do was stretch the truth a little, which is exactly what he had done to me. So fuck him. He had it coming.

Someone stepped right in my line of sight and I almost snapped. I could feel the sweat on my brow, the blood rushing to my face. I clenched my teeth until my head shook and swore under my breath. I moved the camera around, playing with the zoom, until Richards and our leading man reappeared. All was not lost. They were still only talking.

And then it happened. Everything fell right into place. Vicky's friend slid himself over in the booth, so close their legs had to be touching. What threw me was Richards didn't move. Not only did he not move, he seemed to welcome the approach. Then he closed his eyes and his mouth dropped open. I couldn't believe what I was seeing. Our leading man had his hand under the table. You could tell he was using it by the action of his shoulder. He was looking right at Richards, inches away, grinning a little, seeming to be happy with himself, pretending to enjoy it. Richards kept his eyes shut. Squeezed them tight and moved his head a little each time our leading man's shoulder pulsed.

I sat back, a stupid look of disbelief plastered all over my face. No way, I thought. There's no way.

I shook my head and laughed. Without meaning to, I called across the table. 'There's no fucking way.'

Two guys standing nearby looked at me like I was crazy and left, which improved my line of sight. I zoomed in.

Richards had the tip of his tongue between his lips. His brow was knit. He was nodding and, it seemed by the increased movement of his shoulders and chest, breathing heavily. Our man leaned in even closer, lips parted.

I couldn't watch, but part of me felt like standing on the table and doing a victory dance full of fist pumps and face-contorted roars. I had him, the son of a bitch. He was doing everything for me. I wouldn't have to edit a God damn thing.

Jesus, I thought. Richards. I never would've guessed. Not that it mattered. I couldn't care less. What I did care about was how he was going to react when I walked over there, showed him my camera, and said something like, 'Two can play at this game, asshole.' He'd flip. How could he not? He sure as hell wouldn't want anyone to see what I'd filmed. I was home free. There was no way he wouldn't do what I wanted.

There was some other guy standing at Richards' table now, his back to the camera, blocking the view. It didn't matter. I had enough. I had the scene.

I pressed stop but nothing happened. I hit it again and still, nothing.

Fuck me.

'Fuck me!'

I shook the camera like I had hold of Richards' neck. I cocked it behind my head, ready to pitch it across the bar, when I felt someone touch my hand and release the camera from my grip. The cops, I thought. Figures. Whatever. Fuck it. I give up. Fuck it all.

But it wasn't the cops. It was Vicky. She sat across from me and set the camera on the table.

'I've worked with fiery directors before, but you take the cake.'

I leaned across the table, my head low, like I was revealing some big secret. 'I didn't press record. Can you believe that? I didn't get any of it and it was perfect. I had him and I didn't press the fuck-ing record button.'

I slapped the table and sat back, laughed and shook my head. I kept shaking my head.

'Does it really matter?'

'What do you mean, does it really matter? Are you serious? That was the whole point. To catch him on camera. To do to him what he did to me.'

'I thought the plan was to blackmail him.'

'Well. Yeah.'

'So you don't really have to have the video. You just need to make him think you do.'

'What if he calls me on it? I need to be able to play the hand.'

She slid her phone across the table. 'I guess it's a good thing I was your second.'

I picked up the phone. A big play button in the middle of the screen. I touched it and there it was, the whole scene recreated.

I could've kissed her. I could've leapt across the table, wrapped my arms around her, and kissed her.

I hit pause, set the phone down, and shook my head. 'I owe you my life.'

'That's quite a debt.'

'You really should start a business.'

'I'd need a good name.'

'The Players Private Eye.'

'Vicky Fern, PPE—I like it.'

I collected the phone from the table. 'May I borrow this?'

'Consider it part of the service.'

I grinned. 'Time to make the stricken deer go weep.'

·   ·   ·

The other guy standing at Richards' table—the guy who had walked into my frame with his back to the camera—didn't react the way I would've reacted had someone grabbed me by the shoulder, pushed me out of the way, and told me to fuck off if I didn't mind.

Instead, he crossed his arms, looked at me, and said my name. I didn't acknowledge him. I was focussed on Richards who was leaning back in the booth, eyes closed, a sick, self-satisfied little grin on his face, both arms stretched across the top of the seat cushions like Hefner with his arms around two blondes. Except there were no blondes, only our man of the hour, and he had removed himself from the booth altogether, having purposefully distanced himself, I could only assume, from the drunken, post-coital Richards.

It was all I could do not to drive my fist straight into his face.

'Hey, Terry.'

He didn't react.

I set my hands on the table, leaned in, and yelled. 'Hey! Terry!'

He opened his eyes, but slowly. I straightened and waited for the lump to come to. I needed him conscious.

'Ben? Is that really you?'

It was the other guy again. This time it registered that he was saying my name. I turned and looked.

'Wyatt?'

What were the odds?

'What the hell are you doing here?'

'I think it would make more sense for me to ask you that question.'

Wyatt and our man of the hour were on either side of me. We formed a sort of triangle with me at the top, sitting-slash-leaning against the table, my back half-turned to Richards.

'I'm here for that asshole.' I jabbed a thumb over my shoulder.

'Maybe you can explain a few things then.'

'I doubt it. Me and explanations haven't had a very good relationship lately.'

'Well, if you're here for him—whatever the reason—maybe you can tell me what the hell he was doing with Sam.'

I assumed Sam was our man of the hour. Then it clicked. They were together.

'Listen, Wyatt. It didn't mean anything.'

'What do you mean, it didn't *mean* anything.'

I shrugged. 'It didn't mean anything.'

'How could it not mean anything?'

'Simple. I paid him to do it.'

Wyatt looked at me. 'You what?'

'It was a gig.'

'A gig?'

He was disgusted. I could tell. He looked at Sam.

'What are you, some kind of fucking whore?'

Sam hung his head. I tried to explain.

'It's not like that. I needed someone to help me frame this lump of shit.' I jabbed a thumb at Richards again. 'Vicky arranged for your man here to play the part.' Smiling, I looked at Sam and clapped. 'And can I tell you, what a performance. Award-winning.'

'Vicky's involved?'

'Hello, Wyatt.'

Vicky touched his shoulder. She must have been watching from the other table and could sense where things were going.

Wyatt looked at her. 'How could you?'

'It didn't mean anything, Wyatt. Really. It was just acting.'

Wyatt crossed his arms. 'Acting.'

'Ben needed someone. Sam's an actor. He was playing a part. It didn't mean anything.'

Wyatt shook his head. 'Everything means something.'

Vicky dug into her bag of characters and pulled out the couples' counsellor. 'Listen. You two were meant for each other. This will all blow over.'

The word 'blow' threw me.

Wyatt shook his head. 'I don't know.'

Sam stepped forward and hugged him. Wyatt didn't resist. I shook my head and returned my attention to Richards. His eyes were barely open and his arms were still slung around the invisible blondes.

I reached across the table and slapped him. 'Wake up, you son of a bitch.'

He gave his head a little shake and tried to focus on me.

'Well, would you looky there. Benjamin Dunn.'

'That's right, asshole.'

'What're you doing here?'

'What am I doing here?'

'That *is* what I asked.'

'Oh, you know. It was opening night for this little play I wrote.'

'A playwrite. I had no idea, Ben. Congratulations. And what's your little play about?'

'Revenge.'

He blinked hard a few times, brought his arms down and sat forward. Groaned and sighed heavily.

'Revenge?'

'Don't play dumb, Richards.'

He was squinting at me now, more focussed. He shook his head. 'I'm sure I don't have the slightest idea' —hiccup— 'what you're talking about.'

'You set me up, you fuck, and then you knocked me down.'

'I never set you up. And to be clear, you knocked yourself down.'

'You ruined me. You're the reason I was fired.'

He grinned. I nearly hit him.

'I wasn't the reason, Benjamin. You were.'

'Listen, I never sold any drugs to any God damn student.'

I slammed a fist on the table. He sipped the end of his most recent triple Scotch.

'I have a video that says otherwise.'

'Well I have a video that says you pay men to jerk you off in bars. How do you like that?'

He looked at everyone standing around me. I could see the slow connections being made in his eyes.

'That's right. Patricia Duncan's an actor. Her real name is Vicky Fern. Remember it. She'll be famous one day and you can say you knew her when. You can tell everyone how she tricked you into thinking you won the Governor General's Award. You self-righteous, egotistical prick.'

I turned to look at Vicky. She gave him a finger wave. Wyatt and Sam were standing beside her, holding hands. Her talents were limitless.

I looked at Richards again. 'Yup. He's an actor, too. The guy you paid for sex. The other guy's his boyfriend and he's pretty pissed. So I'd tread lightly if I were you.'

Richards shook his head and let out a nervous laugh. 'I never paid him.'

'Well. I've got you on camera paying the waiter for your drinks. A little editing and it's you paying Sam here for a hand job.'

'Wait a minute' —this was Sam— 'you never said anything about making me look like that. Vicky told me it would look like a scene from a film, that I could use it for my web page.'

I turned. Vicky whispered something to Sam and he looked reassured. I returned to Richards. He crossed his arms.

'You wouldn't dare.'

I grinned and thought of Chantal. 'Oh, yes, I would.'

'It's not just me you'd be smearing. What about him?' He looked past me to Sam.

'His reputation means nothing to me.'

I could hear Vicky trying to control Sam behind me. I could hear Wyatt too.

'Looks like it means something to them.'

'That's not my concern. Now listen. If you don't do what I ask, I'll upload this video' —I showed him the phone and set it on the table— 'title it Richards' Reunion with Student and send it to every teacher at Heron River. I'll make sure Eckerton is first on the list. I'll send it to the Board, the PTA, the Rotary Club, the Town Council. It'll ruin you.'

He shook his head. 'I don't think you will.'

I crossed my arms and leaned back. 'Try me.'

'There isn't an ounce of truth in it.'

'There doesn't have to be. You should know that.'

Sam and Wyatt were still arguing with Vicky behind me.

Richards said, 'What do you want?'

'It's simple. I want you to go to Eckerton and the police and the Board and tell them—no, *insist*—that I didn't sell drugs to any student. I want you to tell them you doctored the video to make it look the way it did.'

'But I didn't.'

'I don't care. That's not the point.' I leaned forward and slammed the table again. 'The point is I didn't sell any fucking drugs to any fucking student.'

He tipped his glass back and made a sucking sound.

'I want my name cleared. I want apologies written. I want my license reinstated. In short, I want justice to be done.'

He smirked at me. 'Justice was done.'

'You know what? Fine.' I made a show of bringing the video up on the phone. 'I'm sending it right now.'

I thumbed a few actions into the keypad.

'How do I upload this, Vicky?' I turned and held the phone up towards her. I felt Richards grab my arm.

'Okay. Okay. I'll do it.'

At the same moment I felt another hand take the phone from me. I turned, expecting to see Vicky. But it was Wyatt. His eyes were full of hate. He held the phone between his forefinger and thumb like it were a match he'd struck and was now dangling it above a line of gasoline snaking the distance from him to me where I was tied to a barrel set to explode.

I looked at him. *Come on, Wyatt. It's me. Ben. I wouldn't do anything to hurt you or anyone close to you. You know that. Please. Please don't do this. I've got him. Don't you see? I've got the son of a bitch exactly where I want him. Let me finish him. Please.*

He grinned like he understood. The years and years of knowing each other had allowed for wordless communication. Relief poured in. However badly I'd treated him, there was still a history of friendship between us, the kind of history that didn't just disappear, the kind of history that prevented him from dropping the match.

I smiled and reached for the phone. Still grinning, he let go. Time slowed. I heard the phone hit the floor. I watched him lift his foot and hold it there. I cried out for him not to but it didn't matter. I couldn't undo what I'd done. He drove his heel into the tiny screen and all the little mechanisms of revenge and communication crunched to a halt.

Richards laughed when Wyatt's heel came crashing down onto the face of the phone, and that was it. I stood, incensed, and pushed my way through the bodies around us. Until then, no one had paid any attention to us. The place was too packed, too loud, and we were nothing but another group of good and bad. I was like Hamlet with the sword at the end.

But now I had the attention of the court. I had an audience. I was shoving strangers and screaming unintelligibly. I took a table in my hands and flipped it. I punched someone in the stomach without looking at him and he buckled over. Another man grabbed me. I took his wrist and threw him to the ground. I stole a drink from a nearby table and offed it in a single gulp. Some of the poison ran from the corners of my mouth and I used my sleeve to wipe it. I turned and brought the laughing Richards into sight. I stood there, chest heaving like a monster, and zeroed in. Everyone around me cleared the way and watched. I clomped towards him—that piss-ant sitting there in his booth of debauchery like a black-hearted, bloated king—drew back my fist, and in one fluid, focussed action—unclouded by any pale cast of thought—I cold-cocked him.

Bam. Right in the kisser.

The Rest

In the end, being set up and forcibly removed from Heron River High School was the best thing that could've happened to me. The word 'best' is relative, of course—it is true only in the context of itself. But it really was the best thing that could've happened. I never would've had the courage to leave on my own. I would've been stuck. Stupid to think of it as 'stuck,' I know. But honest.

I can see Big Joe's hands reaching across the Atlantic to choke me. I tease him and laugh because he can't quite get a grip. I can see Norman Scott, too, standing on the distant shore beside Joe, hands like a megaphone at his mouth, shouting with everything he has, 'Don't. Be. An idiot.' I smile to myself and think, Too late.

.   .   .

I wish I could go back to the last time I saw you. Standing in the street in the snow outside your shop on Upper George's Street. When you stepped in and kissed me and then walked away. The slow snow in the light of the street falling all around you. I'd stop you if I could go back. I'd stop you from leaving. But not physically. I'd say something to make you stay. I wouldn't run after you and grab you the way I did. I didn't mean for you to fall. It was an accident. It was the snow. It was slippery. I scared you. I know. I could see it in your eyes. I can still see the way you looked at me. I wish I could undo that most of all. It's all I see when I think of your face. Your fear of me. You rubbing your wrist. Looking up at me from the snowy street, looking away. Stiffening when I went to help you up. Like an animal afraid of its captor. The cold word dropping like a stone repeatedly in my head. *Don't*. The angry echo of it. *Don't. Don't*. That was the moment. I know it now like I knew it then. Why I ran after you and grabbed you like that I'll never know. I was upset. I couldn't

believe you were just going to leave. I wish I could undo it. I
wish I could go back there, to that street and that time. When you
stepped in and kissed me and then walked away. The slow snow
falling all around. I'd call after you and tell you I knew Reilly was
my son. You'd stop and turn. I'd tell you I knew as soon I saw the
picture tucked in the corner of the mirror in your shop. I knew
as soon as I saw his eyes that he was yours. And the look he had,
the way one corner of his mouth went up a little higher when he
smiled. I knew he was mine. There was no way he wasn't.

My whole life I was a son who was no son. Now I'm a father
who is no father. All I want is to make it right.

.   .   .

So. That's it. That's all I have. The rest has been pretty quiet.
I'm here in Dun Laoghaire in a bar I bought with the money my
father kept in a tin box under his bed. I can only hope he would
have approved. Maybe even been proud. Although I doubt he'd
ever say it. Saying it wouldn't matter though. I'd be able to tell.
With certain things, certain people, words are not necessary. You
just know. And knowing is enough. Maybe he would've sold the
house on Railway Street and joined me here. He would've liked
it, I think. The harbour. The sea. The fishing boats. The shops.
The music. The life in the voices and the streets. He could've set
himself up in a little place to do his wood working. He would've
made chairs for old men to rock in on their patios and porches
smoking their pipes and sipping their Scotch and tea. He
would've been happy. Maybe he would've been. I think you
would've liked him. He would've loved you.

.   .   .

Maybe you'll read this one day and forgive me. Maybe
you'll read it and think a boy deserves a father and a father
deserves a son.

(*Aside.* Deserve *has* got something to do with it.)

.   .   .

Maybe you'll walk in one night and step up on stage. I'll be at the bar pouring pints, wiping glasses, conversing with the regulars. We'll be on about Yeats or fishing or why we think there is no God or why there is. Your voice through the speakers will turn me midsentence. The conversation will end and it won't matter one way or the other. I'll fold my arms and lean against the bar. I'll smile like I was expecting you. Your voice will fill the room and I will close my eyes as you sing of the valley fair. Of the little place you know there. Far in the valley shade. Of the cabin we will build there of clay and wattles made. Of how we will arise and go there. And begin the rest of our days.

.   .   .

Until then maybe I'll take up making things from wood. A bookshelf to start. A rocking chair. If I stay with it long enough, and really learn how, perhaps a little boat to keep at a dock, putter around in, cast a line from. Or a guitar, from the hollow body of it out. I'll try my hand at the music again. Play songs I write on guitars I make. Finally make it big. Like Johnny Cash. Imagine.

There's no sin in that.

Thank you—

Mom (Patty Madill). For believing. For the selfless years of giving. For the home you made us. For the home you gave us. For everything you've done & continue to do. If there is any good in me at all it is because of you.

Stacy Sneath. For being the best sister-friend a brother ever had. For shoring me up when I needed it. For all the quiet support & believing-in & inspiration. And those two beautiful nieces, Carys & Brynn.

Gramma & Poppa (Hazel & William Madill). For showing (not telling) me what it means to work. For all the things I fear I took for granted. For never asking for or expecting a single thing in return.

Dad (Paul Sneath). For the love of language & of books (& the smell of their pages). For the never-too-late time on Galley and the father-son-friendship that followed.

Powell & Sandra Kuchmak. For Tara. For the time in your home to write. For the support. For welcoming me in.

Mr. (Richard) Borek. For teaching me about effort. For teaching me how to think. For teaching me how to write. For teaching me the point to running is not the end.

Di Brandt. For the encouragement. For all the close reading. For taking our work so seriously. For embodying what it means to be a writer and a teacher.

Tom Dilworth. For the real & direct & honest criticism.

Darryl Whetter. For introducing me to Richler (in print). For the time taken and the kind words.

Meira Cook. For the time and effort you took for a stranger. For the thoughtfulness.

Chris Needham. For all the work. For taking a chance. For making this real.

Doug Green. For the confidence & the friendship. For Tenesse to Windsor and beyond. For being a fan of haiku.

Brad Frenette. For the Hinterland. For the scripts. For all the time & all the attempts in Windsor & Toronto. For sharing the will to do.

Brent Cotton. For the conversation. For the lines cast. For the pints raised.

Justin Kouba. For the treks and the adventure. For all the apprenticeship. For being like a brother.

Ethan. My best buddy old pal.
Penelope. My Penny Grace. My princess.
Abigael. My little Rosie Girl. My little rose.
You are my three reasons, my life. You have my whole heart. You always will.

And Tara. My first reader. My love. For the ineffable mother you are. For the incomparable partner you are. For showing an interest in javelin. For all the days we share. For all the moments. For life. Reach for my hand now. Call me in.